A Wallflower Under the Mistletoe

A Wallflower Under the Mistletoe

WALLFLOWERS AND ROGUES

CHRISTMAS WALLFLOWERS
BOOK THREE

DAWN BROWER

You must be the best judge of your own happiness.

— JANE AUSTEN, EMMA

Contents

Prologue

Miss Agatha Cartwright stared out the window watching snow fall from the sky. It had been snowing for several minutes, and a small white blanket had started to form on the cold ground. She turned away from the window and glanced around her tiny bedchamber. It was a sparse room. Her father, Baron Cartwright, had not believed in living frivolously. She had no creature comforts. Sometimes she thought she was lucky to have a blanket to keep her warm at night. If clothing hadn't been a necessity that might have been denied to her too.

This room spoke volumes about the lifestyle she'd had to live. There were not decorations filling the room. The walls were stark white, and the floor a polished wood that had seen better days. The floorboards were dark and needed to be replaced. Her bed was only big enough to fit her small frame. The blanket was a patchwork creation made from old clothes that could no longer be worn. She'd made it herself—so she supposed she wouldn't have that if she hadn't learned to sew with some of the ladies at the vicarage.

Her mother had died in childbed. Agatha had never known her. Perhaps if she had lived there would have been more kindness in her life. Now at four and ten, she had to leave everything she'd known, but she supposed that might be for the best. Nothing in her home had been welcoming. The baron had never liked her, and didn't keep those feelings to himself. He told her often that she was a worthless child that should have died with her mother that day.

She feared he might end her life, and that he secretly hoped she take ill and die to save him the trouble. The irony was that happened to the baron instead. He caught a random fever and died less than a sennight later. Now she was an orphan, and had no one to see to her care. What would happen to her? She couldn't stay in her home any longer. The new baron would take over the household soon and then she'd be homeless. He wouldn't want to care of her…

Agatha had always felt alone in the world. So this didn't change much, but it still hurt to accept it. If she were older perhaps it wouldn't terrify her as much. No, that was a lie. It would not matter what age she was, the unknown would always frighten her. She hated surprises, and she especially disliked not having any control in her life. She would find a way through this, and she made a vow to herself. One day she would do as she pleased and no one would ever tell her what to do again.

"Miss Agatha," a maid said from behind her.

The servants had always been nice to her. They understood her better than anyone else had. Her father had treated them better than he ever did her. So they tried to make up for his horrid behavior. They couldn't do much though. At least they never beat her. "Yes, Beth?" Agatha asked.

"There is a gentleman here to see you." She fidgeted in the doorway. "A fancy one."

Agatha pushed her eyebrows together. Who could possibly be there to see her? She didn't socialize except at church or on the days her father forced her to volunteer with the poor. "Did he tell you why he is here?" or who he was?

"He didn't," she said. "He insisted on seeing you."

She didn't want to meet with him. Agatha had learned a long time ago that stalling the inevitable never solved anything though. It was best to get the unpleasantness out of the way and move forward. "Where is he now?"

"He's in the blue salon," she said. "Should I bring tea?"

Agatha shook her head. If they served refreshments the gentleman might stay longer than she wished him too. Besides she shouldn't offer what didn't truly belong to her. She had her clothes, and the quilt she'd sewn herself. Nothing else was hers. "I do not believe that will be necessary." Agatha moved away from the window. "I'll see him now."

"Yes, miss," Beth said, then left her alone.

She glanced out the window one last time, then left her bedchamber. There was no comfort in there anyway. She doubted she'd know comfort if it bit her. And what a thought that was… A bite would be unpleasant at best. What did that say about her that she'd compared comfort to it? That she had an acerbic view on life? She supposed she did.

If she was going to meet with a fancy gentleman she should make herself presentable. She sat at her sitting table and squinted to check her appearance in the looking glass. It was small and cracked, but serviceable. Her dark hair was pinned back but a few strands had escaped the pins. She tucked them back into place. Dark circles rimmed her green eyes making the color pop against her pale skin.

She didn't look that attractive, but she never had. Agatha had put off this meeting long enough. She stood and left her bedchamber and headed toward the salon. A gentleman was indeed there waiting. He wore all black, from his breaches, to his waistcoat and jacket. His hair was dark too, and his eyes a similar shade as hers. She didn't make much of that. Agatha had always favored her mother from what she'd been told. That was one of the reasons her father hated her. She reminded him of what he'd lost. "Hello, my lord," she said and curtsied. "What may I do for you?"

He frowned and glanced at her as if he were trying to understand her. His gaze met hers and he tilted his head to the side. "Do you like living here?" he asked.

How was she to answer that? Should she speak the truth or tell him what most thought she should say? She chose to be honest. "Not particularly. Why do you ask?"

He grinned. "You're cheeky," he said.

She waited. Agatha had never spoken out of turn before. She expected a dressing down of some sort but none came. "Should I act in a different manner?" She was testing the man and didn't understand why she felt as if she could.

"I expect you to be yourself," he said. "But there are times when a person must be more circumspect. Do you know the difference?"

Agatha considered what he was asking her. "Some social niceties should be observed, but not at the risk of destroying a part of myself."

He nodded. "I've come to take you home with me. I couldn't before your father died," he began. "He would never have allowed it, but I promised your mother I would always look after you. Until now I haven't been able to keep that promise to her. I want to see it right."

"Why would you do that?"

"Because your mother has always been important to me," he answered honestly. "I'm the Duke of Wharton, and from this moment on I'll be your guardian. I have a daughter and I wouldn't want her to be left alone in the world." He waited a moment. "You don't have to live at my estate if you don't wish to. I can make other arrangements if you prefer."

He was a duke… He had to have an enormous estate. "Where would I go instead?" She should know what other choices she had before she made a decision.

"A boarding school," he told her. "Even young ladies should be educated, and I suspect your father didn't believe that. Do you read?"

She shook her head. "Father didn't bother with any sort of education." Her father barely did the smallest things for her. Education was so far above that…

"Then either way we will rectify that and see you learn everything you should, or want to." He smiled. "What would you like to do Miss Agatha?"

She considered everything he'd said. What did she want to do? She might have more freedom if she were to go away to school. That didn't sound like she'd enjoy it though. "Will I have my own room at your estate?" She thought about the barren room she'd had for her entire life.

"You'll have a room in the same wing as my daughter, Seraphina," he told her. "You'll take lessons with her once your education is caught up to hers, and we will have new clothes made for you. Whatever you decide that will be one of my priorities." He glanced over her dress. "That gown has seen better days."

Agatha had repaired it several times already… She jutted her chin out and met his gaze. "I think I'd prefer going to your estate." She hoped she didn't regret that decision. His daughter might be horrid and make Agatha's life miserable.

"Wonderful," he said. "Then we shall depart immediately. Is there anything you wish to pack? Is all of your gowns so threadbare?"

She only had one other gown, and it was far worse. "Yes, Your Grace." Now that she knew he was a duke she addressed him properly. "All my clothing is like this. I only have one item I wish to gather from my room if that is all right." It was a miniature of her mother that she'd hidden away.

"Go retrieve it. I'll wait for you." The duke nodded at her.

Agatha rushed up to her bedchamber and gathered the miniature and put it in her pocket. Then as an afterthought she took her quilt too. She didn't want the duke to know about the miniature, and the quilt would hide that fact from him. The miniature was her little secret. Perhaps one day she'd share it with someone else, but that day was not now. She folded the quilt and went back to the salon.

The duke met her gaze. "Is that all you wish to bring with you?"

She nodded. "I'm ready to depart now."

"Then let's be off. It's several days ride by carriage to the estate," he told her. "Then when the season opens I must return to London. You and Seraphina will accompany me."

She'd never been to London… Agatha had a new life ahead of her and she didn't know what to think about it all. "That sounds…lovely."

They went to the duke's carriage and he helped her inside. It was cold and she was grateful she'd grabbed the quilt. She unfolded it and wrapped herself inside of it and settled into her seat. Not long after that she fell asleep, content for the first time in her life.

TWO YEARS LATER…

Agatha sat in the library reading one of her favorite books. In the two years since she'd come to live with the Duke of Wharton her education had helped her learn a lot about herself. She had many interests now. She loved learning about history and geography. She read many travel books that outlined exotic lands and the animals that lived there. If she could, she'd travel the world and explore it all—if only she'd been born a man and given the freedom to do as she pleased.

The duke had taken care of everything she could possibly need. He had even set up a dowry for her. When Seraphina was launched into society, Agatha would be too. She had no desire to marry any man. The duke had told her if after three seasons she still felt that way he would allow her to travel as she liked—with a proper escort. Agatha lived for that day and studied everything she could. But not everything she read was for preparation for what she believed would be an inevitability. She also read books for pleasure—like the one she read now.

"There you are," Seraphina said from the doorway. Her red hair was plaited elegantly on top of her head. Seraphina was six months younger than Agatha, but she hadn't suffered one day in her life. She hadn't understood how to relate to Agatha at first, but she had tried and that mattered to her. They were as close as sisters now.

"I haven't been hiding," she said. "Did you need me for something?"

"Bas is here," Seraphina said. She wrinkled her nose. "And he's brought friends."

Bas—Sebastian Gray, the Earl of Somerset, was Seraphina's cousin. He'd come to live with the duke at a young age—he was several years older than Seraphina and Agatha. Though most of the time he had been away at school. Now though, he was home more often than not. He had finished all the schooling years ago and hadn't bothered with college. Eton hadn't been enjoyable for him and learning had been difficult.

"Not them…" Agatha wrinkled her nose.

Bas had two friends, the Duke of Riverdale and Marquess of Huntington. Those two were constantly with Bas, and the duke tended to irritate Seraphina. They did not get along well at all. Agatha was secretly glad they were there though. She liked both young gentlemen and they humored her. Agatha tended to ask a lot of questions and most men wouldn't deign to answer her.

"Yes, them," Seraphina said. "Please come with me. Father ordered me to be nice and entertain them." She rolled her eyes. "As if they need me to be there."

Agatha placed a ribbon in her book and closed it, then set it on a nearby table. She could always read later. Seraphina needed her. "Of course I'll come with you." She smiled at her. "Where are we going?"

"To the game room." She frowned. "They wish to play charades of all things. I hate charades."

Agatha didn't particularly like it either. "Perhaps we can suggest a different sort of entertainment…"

"I'll let you make the suggestions. They're more likely to listen to you, then me."

"Very well," Agatha agreed. "I'll think of something."

They entered the game room. The three young gentlemen were already there. Two of them were at the billiards table. Bas and Riverdale were engrossed in a game. Riverdale glanced up and glared at Seraphina. "Did you make time out of your busy schedule to grace us with your presence?" he asked.

"I would never be so rude," Seraphina said. "If I promised to do something I wouldn't ignore it for your sake, your grace."

Agatha had to step in before this took a bad turn. It was already heading in the wrong direction. "The Duke of Wharton asked us to join you for some entertainments. But if you wish for us to leave…"

"Don't be ridiculous," Bas said. "We would never ask you to leave. Come join us." Riverdale glared in his direction, but Bas either pretended not to see him or didn't care.

Agatha sighed and spared a glance at Seraphina. "I thought they wanted to play charades."

"That was father's suggestion," she admitted not at all sounding repentant either.

"Why don't we do something a little more interesting," Huntington said. He had a wicked gleam in his eyes.

Agatha had forgotten he was there, but she had always tried to ignore his presence as much as possible. She glanced in his direction and sucked in a breath. He was as gorgeous as she remembered. She didn't want to notice, but she wasn't dead. His brown hair was streaked with gold and his eyes were a brilliant amber—the same shade as the whiskey the Duke of Wharton preferred to drink.

"What do you propose?" Agatha asked him in a neutral tone. Somehow, much to her amazement, she managed to speak without stuttering. She *hated* how he made her feel.

"A game of hide and seek," he said, then

grinned. "There has to be a lot of places to hide in this castle."

"I like it," Riverdale said. "Four of us can hide, then the other one will try to find us."

"Who will be our seeker first?" Bas lifted a brow.

"I'll go first," Agatha volunteered. She didn't like the idea of this game that much. Hiding in dark places reminded her too much of her childhood and the times she'd been locked in her wardrobe. It had been one of her father's favorite punishments for her.

"No," Seraphina said. "We're not playing this." She knew what Agatha had gone through. They had no secrets from each other.

Agatha placed her hand on Seraphina's arm. "It's all right," she told her. She silently pleaded with her to not make things more difficult than they had to be.

Bas glanced between them. He seemed to see more than Agatha wanted him to. He had always been perceptive. "We should play cards instead."

"We have uneven numbers," Huntington reminded him. "It's this or charades. Pick one."

Everyone groaned. "Go hide," Agatha ordered. "I'll give you a quarter hour until I start looking.

The first of you I find has to look for the other three." She had no wish to play longer than absolutely necessary.

They all stopped arguing and left the room. No room in the castle was off limits, except the duke's private chambers. Agatha sat down and watched a nearby clock. She gave them a little extra time, but not for them. She was mentally preparing herself. Then she started wandering the halls. She started with the library because it was her favorite room. No one was in there of course. Then she walked down the connecting hallway and ended up in the ballroom. It was shrouded in darkness, but she could almost imagine what it must be like filled with candlelight and dancers. It would be magical.

She swirled around the floor as if she were waltzing with an experienced partner. She should be looking for those hiding, but she was in no hurry. She closed her eyes and twirled until she bumped into someone. Agatha gasped.

"It's all right," a gentleman said. "I have you." His voice was husky against her ear.

"Lord Huntington…" Only one man made her heart skip a beat with such efficiency.

"It seems as if you've found me," he said. He seemed pleased with that outcome.

She froze. Agatha didn't know what to make of this. Had he wanted her to find him? "I…" She cleared her throat. "I think it's you that's found me."

Agatha could barely make out his face in the shadows. He smiled. "That might be true too. Either way the game is over isn't it?" Huntington stepped closer to her. Heat suffused her from head to toe.

She nodded dumbly. He confused her, but she didn't want to explore those feelings too deeply. If she did she might start hoping for something that was too far out of reach for her. She was going to travel the world, not become a marchioness. *And why had that thought popped into her stupid head?*

The Marquess of Huntington hadn't offered for her and never would. He wasn't for her either way. There was no room for silly thoughts and wishful-ness. "We should go back to the game room then."

"Yes," he said. His tone held an odd edge to it, almost as if he wished he could disagree with her. "You lead the way."

She didn't argue with him. "I'm going to my chamber," she told him. It was his responsibility to locate the others. "Please give my apologies to the others. I'm not feeling well." She was feeling too much and she had to escape before those unwanted emotions overwhelmed her.

Agatha reminded herself over and over as she walked away from the marquess that he wasn't for her. If she kept telling herself that, she might make herself accept it too. Agatha was a baron's daughter. A marquess did not marry so far beneath them. She best accept that now and save herself from an inevitable broken heart.

One

Four years later…

Agatha stared out the window of the carriage. She shivered slightly and pulled a blanket over her lap. Winter was not her favorite time of the year. It seemed like all the bad things that had happened to her all occurred during the colder months. She'd been born in a snowstorm. The doctor hadn't been able to get to her mother in time to save her. Her father had died suddenly on a cold February day. Though that part had led to something good. Three weeks after her father's death she'd met the Duke of Wharton and her life had been changed irrevocably. Some might argue her birth wasn't a bad thing, except that had been what killed her mother.

Still… As far as she could ascertain nothing good came out of the cold and traveling during that time of the year was worse. She wished she could have stayed in London, but the duke had insisted they travel to Somerset Abbey for Christmastide. The entire family was going there for the holiday, along with a few others. Friends and acquaintances of the Earl and Countess of Somerset would all travel in the abominable cold to celebrate. The earl was the duke's nephew, and this was the first year he was entertaining as a married man.

Agatha rather liked the countess too. She had come to know her for the first time at a house party during Christmastide a year earlier. Eva—Lady Somerset, was a wonderful woman and a good match for Bas. She was glad he'd found happiness.

"I hope Bas appreciates how much we love him," Seraphina nearly whined. She huddled next to Agatha on the seat. She shivered and yanked on her own blanket. "I swear it's colder than it normally is right now."

"It's not," Agatha said in a dry tone. "It's as cold as it always is this time of the year."

"Bas knows you love him," the duke said in an

absentminded tone. He flipped the page of the book he'd been reading since they left the inn earlier that morning. They had departed just after daybreak. "Complaining is not a good look on a well-born lady." The duke could make a person feel small without saying a word, but when he did speak it aloud it was like a rcopening a festering wound. Seraphina flinched.

"I apologize," she told her father. "I hate that I become so surly when I travel."

"You're not like this all the time when we travel," Agatha said nonchalantly. "Only when you're likely to cross paths with a certain duke when we reach our destination."

The duke lowered his book and pinned his daughter with a glare. "You will not bicker with the Duke of Riverdale during this house party." His gaze didn't waver once. "I need a response. You understand what I'm saying don't you?"

"Yes, father," Seraphina said. Her voice was low and without any inflection in it. She turned her gaze to look out the window.

Agatha glanced at Seraphina. In a lot of ways she was a sister to her. Some thought perhaps they were sisters in truth, if not in name. She'd heard some of the hushed whispers over the years. Many members of the ton wondered about the reason the duke had taken her in as his ward. They speculated about the nature of her birth and if the duke was in fact, her father.

He'd never claimed to be anything other than her guardian. Agatha had never outright asked him either. She did have similar coloring as the duke, but that didn't mean he was really her father. Sometimes she wished the rumors to be true. Her father had never seemed to love her. Perhaps that was the reason why.

Seraphina looked nothing like the duke. She had her mother's coloring. Agatha had studied all the portraits in the gallery, and the late duchess had the same red hair and pale blue eyes as her daughter. The duke's eyes were as green as Agatha's. No wonder everyone questioned his motivations regarding her…

She sighed. "Seraphina," she began. "What do you think this house party will be like? Do you believe it will have as much excitement as the one we attended last year?" She had to do something to help Seraphina stop thinking about the Duke of Riverdale. Agatha knew why they always bickered, and the moratorium of that would drive Seraphina mad if she didn't have something else to occupy herself with.

"Doubtful," Seraphina said drolly. "There isn't any scheduled spying this year." She tilted her head to the side and stared at her father. "Or do I have that part wrong?"

"Espionage isn't on the guest list to my knowledge," her father replied without even looking at her. "Nor is smuggling—though that would be quite the feat since there are no secret caves, coves, or even bodies of water that would make it easier to accomplish that endeavor at Somerset Abbey."

"Then whatever shall we do for entertainment?" Seraphina said in a dramatic tone. "I fear we will all suffer constant ennui."

Good. Seraphina seemed to have forgotten all about the Duke of Riverdale. Agatha's task had been successful. "We shall think of something. Eva has probably thought of all of that already. She's excited to be the hostess of this event." They had corresponded quite a bit since they had settled at Somerset Abbey.

"Bas is lucky she agreed to marry him," Seraphina said. "They make each other so happy." She sounded whimsical. Was she thinking about what she didn't or couldn't have? Agatha wouldn't mention any of that. She didn't need Seraphina becoming melancholy.

The carriage turned and the scenery outside changed. It was a long cobbled driveway. "We're almost there," Agatha said. She'd never been to Somerset Abbey, but this had to be the entryway to the estate.

"It's about time," Seraphina exclaimed. "I hope the abbey isn't drafty. I don't know if I'll ever get warm again."

Agatha kept her thoughts to herself. She huddled farther underneath the blanket so her shaking hands were not visible. The cold didn't play any part of her dilemma, though she had experienced far warmer days. No, she had something far more troubling on her mind, or she should say someone. In a few short weeks she would be one and twenty, and not long after that, if she wished, she could travel the world as the duke had promised. No one had offered for her, and she'd have said no if a gentleman had. There was only one man that had ever interested her, and he hadn't given her any indication he wanted to marry her. That didn't stop her from wanting him—the Marquess of Huntington kept his distance, and it hurt deep down every time she felt the brunt of his apathy.

This party would be difficult because he'd be there, but at the end she'd return with the duke, and come spring she'd finally do what she'd always wanted. Maybe then she could forget about the marquess and her troublesome feelings.

ROARKE JAMES, THE MARQUESS OF HUNTINGTON stared at the billiard table and frowned. "How…" He shook his head. "That's impossible."

"It isn't," the Duke of Riverdale said. "That my friend is skill, and I have more than you."

"That's debatable," Roarke drawled. He didn't deny that his friend was good at the game. They had both been playing for years, but clearly Riverdale had been practicing some new moves. "What this tells me is you have more time on your hands than you should." He leaned against the table and met Riverdale's gaze. "Tell me the truth. You're in a dry spell aren't you?"

Riverdale scoffed. "Of course not…" He glanced toward the doorway. The Earl of Somerset strolled in.

"Am I interrupting?" Somerset asked.

"Not at all," Riverdale told him. "I've already trounced Huntington. Do you care to give it a go?"

"At trouncing Huntington?" Somerset lifted a brow. "Hasn't he been humiliated enough?"

Riverdale snorted with laughter. At least the duke had something to laugh about. He'd been in a constant dark mood of late. Roarke didn't know what was bothering him and didn't pry. When Riverdale was ready to talk about it he would.

"Ha, ha," Roarke said in a sardonic tone. "I'm an excellent billiard player." He felt ridiculous defending his skill at the game, but what else was he to say. "Riverdale has learned some new moves though. I think he's hired a tutor."

"I have not," the duke protested. "You're a sore loser. There's nothing else going on here."

They had gathered at Somerset Abbey for the Christmastide season. Roarke and Riverdale had come earlier than the rest of the guests to settle in before they were bombarded. It was the first time they'd been alone with Somerset since his marriage. They rarely got to spend time together anymore. Roarke was happy for Somerset, but also a little jealous. He didn't think he could ever settle down with a woman and find that sort of contentment. If he did there was only one lady he'd want to make his, and she showed no interest in him. "You're right about one thing," Roarke said. His tone held a hint of amusement. "I do not like losing, and I don't often find myself in a situation where I do."

"Which is why this surly attitude of yours is so entertaining," Riverdale drawled. He walked over to a nearby bar and poured two fingers of brandy, then took a healthy drink of it. "Which reminds me…" He turned toward Somerset. "What sort of entertainments are planned for this house party?"

Somerset shrugged. "Other than a Christmas Eve ball I don't know. Eva has been working with the housekeeper to plan everything. This sort of thing is not my forte."

"So what you're saying is we will be hiding in the game room for most of the fortnight," Roarke said. To be honest he'd been planning on doing that anyway. He hated socializing, and if he participated he'd have to spend more time with Miss Agatha Cartwright than he wanted to. She unsettled him whenever he was near her.

"I hope not," Riverdale said. "You're surly enough as it is after losing one game." He turned to Somerset and said. "Can you imagine how he'll be if he loses everyday while we're here?"

"It will be all right," Somerset told them. "Eva has thought of everything." He had a reassuring tone as he spoke.

Roarke froze and looked at Somerset. He said carefully, "I thought you didn't know what she had planned." Was there some sort of surprise Somerset didn't want them to know about?

"I don't," he said in a casual tone. "I trust my wife." He shrugged. "You'll understand one day when you find the love of your life. There are some things that you will just know. Trust me."

Roarke did trust Somerset. His wife seemed like a decent sort, but he didn't know her as well as the earl did. He didn't trust easily and wasn't about to start now. He'd have to have a conversation with the countess. Perhaps soon… "When will your uncle arrive?" When will *she* be around to torment him? He had to stop thinking about Agatha.

And if he could do that he would have stopped years ago…

"Today I think," Somerset replied. "If they didn't run into any delays."

Roarke froze on the inside. So soon… He hadn't expected that reply. "Then we better play a few games before he arrives. He'll want to steal all your time, and we all know what that means."

"I'm not doing that anymore," Bas insisted.

"Once a spy always a spy," Riverdale told him. "You might think you're retired, but we all know better. The Duke of Wharton has expectations, and you can never say no to him."

Somerset grinned. "I will. You'll see." He picked up a cue stick. "My wife and the life we have here is more important than pleasing my uncle."

He might actually believe that. Perhaps it was true… Roarke smiled. "You play Huntington. He needs to be taken down and I think you're the man to do it." He leaned against the ledge near the window. "And I plan on watching his downfall."

And try his damn best to pretend he didn't have a care in the world…

Two

Afternoon sunlight streamed through a nearby window and sent illumination throughout the room. Agatha took a sip of her tea and pretended to listen to the conversation around her. They had arrived at Somerset Abbey several hours earlier. Seraphina and Agatha had rested for a bit, but then had come down to join Eva for tea.

So far none of the gentlemen had made an appearance and she hoped they didn't. Dinner would be in a couple of hours and that was too soon for her. She would probably have to sit next to the marquess at dinner. No other guests had arrived and it would be less formal, but still there would be seating arrangements. Eva wanted everything to be perfect, and that meant following the rules of social engagement to the letter.

"These biscuits are wonderful," Seraphina said a little too enthusiastically.

Agatha narrowed her gaze. "Are you being honest?"

"Why wouldn't I be?" Seraphina asked in an innocent tone.

"Because we both know how Bas feels about biscuits," Agatha said. "And when Eva met him he ate them as heartily as you're proclaiming how wonderful they are."

Eva sighed. "He is really picky about his biscuits. I finally convinced the Duke of Wharton's cook to share her recipe with our cook. Since Bas doesn't reside there any longer he'll never have the ones he likes otherwise."

"So this is the recipe he likes so much," Seraphina said. "I thought it might be. They taste familiar." She popped the last bit of one in her mouth and chewed thoughtfully. "I'm not as particular as he is though. My cousin is a bit odd at times."

Eva shrugged. "I wouldn't go that far. I think he's perfect as he is."

"You have to say that," Seraphina declared. "You're his wife."

"She doesn't," Agatha disagreed. "She knows all his darkest secrets and loves him as he is. If she thinks he's perfect, to her, he is. I'm sure if he is wrong about something she'll disagree with him if need be."

Seraphina rolled her eyes. "You don't need to be arbitrary for the sake of it."

"I don't believe I am." Agatha tilted her head to the side. "I like to think I am being fair."

This conversation was beyond silly. She didn't even know why they were discussing it to begin with. What did any of this matter? So Bas was particular about the type of biscuits he liked… many people had idiosyncrasies like that. She didn't know what else they would discuss though. Agatha was still a bit fatigued from their traveling. She was glad they had arrived before most of the guests.

"That will be the sentiment everyone will remember you for," Seraphina said. "Her lies Agatha, she only wanted to be fair."

"You're more surly than usual today," Agatha said thoughtfully. "Why? Has something happened to upset you?" She wouldn't comment on what she'd said. Agatha had always been the sort that wanted to please the people that mattered to her, but she wouldn't do it at her own expense. She'd learned at an early age that it wouldn't serve her to be anything other than who she was deep inside. Being able to see both sides in a situation had always benefitted her.

"I don't know." Seraphina set her teacup down and slumped on the settee. "I just feel…soooo…" She shook her hand trying to find the right word.

"Unsettled?" Eva supplied.

"Maybe," Seraphina replied. "Maybe I'm just still tired from our journey. I don't know."

"I know I am," Agatha said. "Neither one of us has been the sort to enjoy spending days in a carriage." She set her own teacup down. "What can I do to help you?"

"Nothing," Seraphina said exasperated. "It's something I need to work through on my own." She turned to Eva. "I promise I won't be this difficult the entire time. I will be better tomorrow. I hope I won't be this horrid at dinner."

"You should be all right," Eva said. "Don't worry so much."

"She's right, and remember to not let Riverdale goad you." Agatha hoped the duke didn't make

Seraphina more irritated later. "Your father wants this to be an enjoyable holiday."

Seraphina mumbled something under her breath but Agatha couldn't make out the words. She was probably cursing Riverdale's very existence. Agatha could understand if she were. "I won't bait him," Seraphina said through clenched teeth. "But I cannot control what that man does or says. I just pray I don't react badly to any of it."

So did Agatha… "I'm certain you'll be able to manage one meal without giving into the need to dress him down."

"Why do you and the duke loathe each other?" Eva asked. "Bas won't tell me."

"It's a long story…or maybe a short one," Seraphina said. "Either way I don't have the strength to tell it today. I will one day, I promise."

"Why don't I walk you to your chamber," Agatha said. "You can lay down until dinner and help prepare yourself for what a chore it will be."

Eva smiled. "Go," she told them. "We have plenty of time to talk later."

"Oh, all right," Seraphina agreed. "I could use some time alone."

Agatha and Seraphina stood and left the room. It didn't take long to reach Seraphina's bedchamber. Seraphina opened the door and stepped inside. "Do you need anything before I depart?"

Seraphina shook her head. "No," she answered. "Go. I know you are itching to explore the library. This is probably your best time to do it."

Agatha grinned. "Bas promised there were a lot of travel books and maps for me to look over while we visited. I do want to look at them." She nibbled on her bottom lip. "But I don't want to leave you…"

"I'll be all right, I promise," Seraphina told her. "Go look at your boring maps."

She blew out a breath. "Only if you promise to send for me if you need anything."

"There are servants for that," Seraphina reminded her. "I shouldn't need you."

"Still…" Agatha knew what it was like to be abandoned by the people that were supposed to care for her. It was something that she couldn't let go of—even though the duke had been nothing but kind and considerate since she'd come to live with them. "Promise me."

"I vow it," Seraphina said. "I will be fine. Now go." She shooed her out the door.

Agatha left her and went down to find the library. She had been waiting to find the books and maps Bas had told her about. At least those should be reliable. People couldn't always be counted on.

ROARKE HAD LEFT SOMERSET AND RIVERDALE alone in the game room hours earlier. He'd wandered up to his bedchamber and relaxed with a book, but now that he'd finished it he needed another one. He was one of those odd sorts that would rather spend time with a good book then people. He'd had enough socializing earlier, and now he'd rather be by himself. Especially since he would have to converse and be sociable at dinner.

For now he'd return the book to the library and find something else to read. Hopefully no one would be in the room to bother him. The library was usually empty, and for that he had been grateful. The only time it seemed as if people wandered into the room was to have some sort of tryst. He hated that it was the first place lusty couples went to satisfy their needs. Couldn't they find some other dark room to copulate in?

He pushed open the door and entered the library. There was a nice fire in the hearth and sunlight streamed through the windows. It was a well lit room and inviting. A woman with dark hair and a light green dress stood near the desk. She leaned over to study something laid out before her. Whatever it was must be fascinating. She hadn't noticed him walk into the room.

Roarke strolled over to her and leaned against the side of the desk. Still she didn't notice him. He didn't know how that made him feel. Normally he would leave her be, but he couldn't resist the temptation she laid before him. "Agatha," he said her name softly.

She jerked her head up and met his gaze. "Oh, my…" Agatha lifted her hand to her chest. It shook a little as she stared at him. "Make some more noise next time. You frightened me."

"I was not exactly quiet." He lifted a brow. Her green eyes were quite lovely—several shades darker than her dress. "What is this that has your attention?"

"It's a book about the West Indies," she replied. "The travel trade, routes, and places of interest." She trailed her finger over one of the maps drawn in the book. "I often wonder what it must have been like for those that traveled these routes."

"I'm sure it isn't as splendid as you're imagining," he said, then frowned. "A ship is a festering place of rot and filth. The men spend weeks aboard without much opportunity for bathing. It smells…foul."

"I imagine it would if they can't wash properly." She tilted her head to the side. "Does that mean you've traveled before?"

"Of course," he said. "Most young men have had some sort of grand tour to experience the world. Some of it was nice. Some…not so much."

"The smelly ships for instance." Her eyes sparkled a little as she spoke. It nearly sucked the breath right out of him. She was so utterly lovely. He wondered if she realized how beautiful she actually was, and if she did why hadn't she found some lucky gentleman to make hers.

"Among other things…" He frowned. "Why are you looking at all of this?"

"Bas told me he had some books and maps for me to look at. He knows how much I like to read about others traveling exploits." There was a fanciful quality to her tone. Like she wished for something just out of reach.

"Why do you like them?" He shouldn't continue this conversation. Roarke should find a new book and leave immediately. The more he understood her or learned about her, the more he wanted to discover. This was a disaster in the making.

"The duke promised me years ago that if I still did not wish to marry by my twenty first birthday I could travel wherever I liked." She smiled as she looked down at the book. Agatha looked at it as if it were her greatest treasure. "If I am to pick a destination I must learn what I can about the world before I leave." She glanced up at him. "If you had never traveled, where would you choose to go?"

Roarke pushed his eyebrows together. He didn't like the idea of her traveling anywhere in the world. What if she chose to go somewhere dangerous? Who would protect her? It made him uncomfortable to consider about her alone in the world—what was the Duke of Wharton thinking? "Italy is lovely." No matter what he chose it wouldn't ever be safe for her. He should speak to the duke and convince him that this was a horrible idea.

"I've read much about Italy," she said. "It is definitely on my list. Greece seems interesting too. So much history there…" Agatha tapped her chin. He followed the movement with his eyes. Roarke couldn't look away. "But the places in Africa…those seem so wild and untamed. It might be much more interesting there."

His heart stopped inside his chest. She couldn't actually be considering going there. "No," he said.

"No?" She asked in a confused tone. "You don't think it would be like that?"

Oh, it most definitely would… "I mean no, it wouldn't be that interesting. Well." He considered his words carefully. "It might be in parts, but the bad parts would far outweigh the good. Remember the smelly ship…the entire trip would be like that. It would not be comfortable."

"There are many things in life that lack some of the comforts in life. Some people even have to live with them daily." She studied him. "Perhaps, my lord, you're too spoiled."

"No doubt part of that is true," he agreed. "I am aware I live a privileged life, but then again, so do you."

She nodded. "You're right of course. Now I most definitely do, but it hasn't always been that way. I like to think I could live with a lot less if necessary."

He realized then there was much he didn't know about her. What had her life been like before she had come to live with the duke? He was aware of the gossip surrounding her. Many in the top believed her to be one of the duke's by-blows.

Roarke wasn't so sure about that. Would the Duke of Wharton bring his bastard daughter to live with his legitimate one? They were also very close in age. Instead of trying to talk her out of this absurd plan of hers he asked her a different question instead. "When will you be one and twenty?" He needed to know how much time he had left to plan a way to prevent this.

"In one week," she answered. "My birthday is two days after Christmas."

That wasn't nearly enough time. He had a lot to consider. "If I forget," he replied. "Happy early birthday, and I do hope you get everything you wish for." Roarke smiled. "I'll leave you to your studying." With those words he left her alone. He hadn't bothered to find another book. He had something far more important to occupy his time with.

Three

gatha smiled as she strolled down the hallway toward the library. She couldn't help it. Happiness filled her to the brink and threatened to spill over uncontrollably. She couldn't explain it and didn't even want to try. It just was, and she accepted it.

The joy that filled her heart had nothing to do with the people she interacted with and it most definitely did not involve a certain marquess. He had been nice the day before, and had actually seemed fascinated with her wants and dreams. She should not take any of that to heart. Just because he showed her an inkling of kindness did not mean he had any interest in her.

The marquess had never been cruel toward her.

He barely paid her any attention at all. There were times when he spoke to her and his innate benevolence showed then too. He just never showed that side to her with any regularity. Agatha couldn't say with any sort of certainty that he thought about her beyond those brief moments of connection. Any feelings on her part were clearly not returned by him—she had to own her emotions and accept that he would never be hers.

And she was perfectly all right with that…

Her future didn't hold a marriage filled with unrelenting love. She would never have what Eva and Bas had. They had a fairy tale sort of love. The kind where their love was unshakeable and they kept the promises they made each other. That was a rarity, and if she couldn't have even a small amount of that magic—she wanted nothing at all. She'd do what she always said she'd do… Travel the world and see all the wonders it had to offer her. In that she'd find a different sort of magic. That would have to be enough for her.

She reached the library and went inside. Eva had been busy decorating before the rest of the guests arrived. Boughs of holly decorated the walls, and wreathes hung on the walls. Red ribbon had been wound down the staircase, and sometime when Agatha hadn't been paying attention they'd hung mistletoe in random places.

What was Eva thinking?

That was a disaster or scandal ready to happen. Was she hoping to bring a couple together by giving them permission to kiss under the tempting foliage? Agatha would have to avoid the mistletoe as best as she could. The problem of course was that she had a tendency to not pay attention to her surroundings.

The servants were still busy decorating the hallway outside the library. Agatha avoided them as best as she could and slipped inside. She hadn't made a dent in reading the tomes that Bas had plucked off his shelves for her. Her curiosity about other countries was endless, and Bas knew it. He often found different books he thought might interest her. Bas had trouble reading, but he didn't let that stop him from learning all he could too. He understood her better than most did. In some ways he was like the brother she'd never had.

Agatha went straight to the desk. When she reached it she frowned. The book she'd been reading was gone. Where could it be? Had someone taken it? She started to search through all the tomes on the desk and still couldn't locate it. The rest of the books Bas had left for her were there. Only the one she'd been looking at the previous day was missing.

She didn't know what to do. The only person that had known she wanted to read it was Bas, and well…Huntington. He'd found her reading it. When he had been there with her he'd been so attentive. He wouldn't have taken it. Would he? She should find him and ask him. But first…she'd ask one of the servants. Perhaps they'd moved it or seen who had taken it.

Agatha went out into the hallway. "Pardon me," she said to the nearest maid. "Can you assist me?"

"Certainly, miss," the maid said. "What may I help you with?"

"There is a stack of books on the desk in the library," she began. "I had one open on top of the desk." She should have marked her page, but hadn't thought to. "It's missing. Do you happen to know where it might be?"

She shook her head. "No, miss. I haven't been in the library."

"Have you seen anyone else go inside besides me?" Agatha asked. Perhaps that was a better place to start her search.

"Oh, yes," she said enthusiastically. "One of his

lordships friends went in there as we began decorating."

Bas only had two friends currently in attendance. The Marquess of Huntington and the Duke of Riverdale were actually his only two real friends. One of them had her book, and she'd be willing to bet everything she owned it was the marquess. He'd had an odd expression on his face when she'd told him about her plans to travel. She hadn't given it much thought at the time. But on further reflection it should have concerned her.

Huntington, Riverdale, and Bas were known as the shrewd three. At least that is what the Duke of Wharton often called them. That made the marquess a mastermind. One that was comfortable hiding his true motivations. Well, he would give her back her book. She didn't care why he'd taken it as long as he returned it.

"Thank you," she told the maid. "Do you recall where he went after he left?"

She shook her head. "I didn't pay him any mind. The decorations…" She glanced back at her unfinished work.

"Don't worry," Agatha said reassuringly. "It isn't important." It was to her but the maid didn't need to think she'd done something wrong. Huntington was the one that had taken the book. "I'm sorry I've taken you away from your duties. I can see to this myself."

"Yes, miss," the maid said. Then she went back to her task of decorating. Agatha stormed down the hallway in search of a certain marquess.

ROARKE SAT IN ONE OF THE MANY SALONS INSIDE Somerset Abbey and scrolled through the book he'd pilfered from the library. It was the one she'd been flipping through the day before. Agatha had been fascinated with it, and Roarke wanted to under-stand why.

Riverdale and Somerset had gone riding. Roarke had no desire to do that in the bitter cold. He'd much rather stay inside where it was warm and he didn't freeze his bollocks off. He would have to return the book, but a part of him wanted to keep it. Perhaps she would come looking for it. He liked the idea of that. She'd be angry. Agatha rarely lost her temper, but when she did… It was like a pot boiling over.

Someone pushed he door open and it hit the wall with a loud bang. He glanced up and his lips twitched. That pot was past boiling over. Steam was pouring out and all the water had evaporated outward. Agatha was beyond furious. "There you are." Some dark strands had escaped from her normally perfect coiffure and her green eyes were like emerald fire. Her day dress was a simple light green muslin that was more demure than revealing. He found it incredibly alluring though. What the hell was wrong with him?

"You were looking for me?" He casually flipped another page and glanced down. Roarke was doing a remarkable job of pretending to be engrossed in the tome.

"That's mine," she said in an uncompromising tone. "Give it back."

He glanced up at her. Red splotches had filled her cheeks and it could be his imagination but her lips even seemed to darken a shade. It made him think of hot, feverish kisses and lust filled nights. Roarke barely suppressed a groan. "Yours?" he lifted a brow. "I must have been mistaken then, but I thought all the books in the library belonged to the Earl of Somerset."

She blew out a frustrated breath. "They do," she said through gritted teeth. "However, he left the books out on the desk specifically for my use while I am in residence."

"I see," he said, then flipped another page. "Isn't there a whole stack there?"

"Yes…" Agatha narrowed her gaze. "Why does that matter?"

"Because you could browse one of the other ones while I look this one over." Roarke shook his head at her. "I find your attitude disappointing. You always seem so generous in spirit and now you're being difficult because I am using something before you have had a chance to."

Agatha opened her mouth, then closed it. He didn't know what she'd been about to say, but his fascination hadn't ebbed once since she stormed into the room. "You're right," she said finally. "It is horrible of me to deny you the opportunity to read it."

She'd given in far to quickly. Why was she always acting like the peacemaker? "Why do you want this one so much?" he asked.

"I just don't like jumping from one book to another without finishing the one I started first."

He nodded thoughtfully. "My apologies. I didn't mean to distress you." Roarke had wanted to understand her better. That had been his sole reason for taking the book to begin with. The book didn't give him the insight he'd been hoping to find.

"It's all right," she said. All that anger and steam had just melted out of her. Roarke felt like an arse. "Just return it when you've finished. I will go start a different book."

Agatha turned to leave the room and he found himself frustrated. He didn't want her to leave. "Wait," he called out to her. Roarke closed the book and stood to walk over to her. "Don't go."

She stopped suddenly and glanced up at him. He'd taken three long strides to stand in front of her. He'd been this close to her in the past, but for some reason it felt differently now. It was like staring up at the sun and being blinded by it's radiance. He hadn't been able to see through that light and really see her before. Now she glowed, but more subtly. As if she had dimmed her light enough to let him see how special she was, and it swallowed him whole.

"I shouldn't stay," she said. "It's not proper."

"No one will say anything," he told her. "We can create one hell of a scandal and if we wished to keep it to ourselves, the current guests would allow us to."

She lifted a brow. "Do you hope to start a scandal with me then?"

He smiled. She was so damn bloody beautiful and brilliant. This could be dangerous to him. "Not today," he said in a casual tone. "At least not this early. Ask me later."

Her lips twitched as she fought a smile. "I'll try to remember to do that." She shook her head lightly. "What did you need?"

Roarke needed her… God help him. He'd never wanted a woman as much as he did this one. He should let her walk away, but he was finding it far too difficult to allow that. "You should take this now." He held up the book. As he started to give it to her he noticed the mistletoe above her. She glanced up then too.

"Don't," she said.

"Don't what?" he asked. His tone had gone a little hoarse. He had been thinking about kissing her. It would be the perfect excuse to give in to what he wanted. She would even let it go. The mistletoe had made him do it… Surely, he wouldn't do anything so untoward if the greenery hadn't been present.

"You know," she said in a quiet tone. "It would be a mistake."

"But the best of mistakes…" He closed his eyes and took a deep fortifying breath. He had to be stronger than this. If there was ever a woman that would make him want more than his menial life, it would be her. Agatha made him believe in a happy-ever-after. The kind like Somerset had with his wife, and the sort he never believed he would have. "But you are right. We shouldn't go down that road."

"I'm glad we understand each other." She took the book from him. "If you want to read any of the others you can. Just let me know if you take one next time. I can be…"

"Demanding?" he supplied.

"Determined," she said. "I like things in an orderly fashion and when they're out of place it distresses me."

He nodded. "I'll be more considerate next time." He would look over those other books too. Roarke wanted to know what she had planned. There had to be a way to convince her this scheme of hers would end in disaster. He wanted to protect her, and he would do it at whatever cost. The Duke of Wharton would be able to help with that. He couldn't possibly be all right with her traveling, no matter what he said. The duke was a controlling arse.

"Thank you," she said, then turned on her heels to leave.

Roarke watched her go. His hands were clenched at his sides. He'd done it to stop himself from pulling her into his arms and kissing her senseless. It had taken every ounce of his strength to not kiss her. She'd been so delectable it hurt to gaze upon her.

Maybe one day he could kiss her as he dreamed, but Roarke doubted it. A woman like her—she deserved far better than him. He was not a good man, and she was everything a man like him dreamed about.

Four

While Eva had supervised the decorating of the abbey, Agatha and Seraphina had been left alone to amuse themselves. Agatha was grateful for that time, Seraphina—hated it. She wasn't the sort to be left with idle hands. Schedules were made for a reason, and Seraphina adhered to one with all things. She hated spontaneity.

"Maybe Eva needs assistance," Seraphina said for the fifth time.

Agatha glared at her.

"What?" Seraphina said. "She might need help. You never know…"

"We do know," Agatha said. Again. Seraphina could be stubborn at times. "You asked one of the maids and she said they have it all in hand. You'll just have to find something else to occupy your time."

Huntington and Riverdale strolled into the sitting room. Riverdale froze when his gaze landed upon Seraphina. "Of course you're in here," he said.

She rolled her eyes. "If my company is so unappealing perhaps you can find another place to go. Maybe even another estate if that's at all possible."

He stared at her as if she'd grown a second head. "This is my friend's estate. Why would I leave?"

Seraphina laughed. "Because the earl is my family. I think I have a higher standing."

Huntington blew out an exasperated breath. "We can go to another room."

"No," the duke said in a mulish tone. "She can't order us about. I want to stay here."

Agatha almost laughed. He was acting like a spoiled child, and Seraphina wasn't any better. When would those two find a way to get along better? She had to steer Seraphina away from this interaction. Her father would not be pleased with her if he happened upon them.

This was the same sitting room she'd found

Huntington in earlier. Was this a popular place to congregate? There wasn't anything special about the room. It was decorated in dark blue and gold. The settee was comfortable and the matching chairs passably so. She could easily nap there if she thought she'd be undisturbed.

"We can always go into the game room," Huntington said. "You can show me that new move you learned on the billiards table."

"I don't want to play billiards right now. We promised Somerset we'd join him there later." Riverdale kept glaring at Seraphina. "I'm not the one being ridiculous. I can share if she can."

"I don't believe you," she said in a scathing tone. "I'm not the one that entered and made unsavory declarations."

"Seraphina," she said in a soft tone. "Do I need to remind you of the promise you made?"

She tore her angry gaze from the duke and faced Agatha. "No," she said mulishly. "I remember quite vividly what I was tasked to do." She looked as if she was about to stomp her foot in protest, but then it was as if something clicked and her mood changed. Her blue eyes sparkled with mischief and her lips turned upward.

Uh oh…what was she thinking?

"Agatha," she said. "I think we should be the ones to depart. We have been in this room overly long. It's only fair to give them the opportunity to enjoy it."

The last thing she wanted to do was argue with Seraphina. She happily followed her out of the sitting room. Once they were several steps away from the two gentlemen she stopped and grabbed Seraphina's arm. "What are you planning?"

Her lips twitched as she fought a smile. "Why are you so distrusting? I'm not going to do anything scandalous."

"But you are going to do something," Agatha insisted. "He pushed you too far this time didn't he?"

Her smile faded. "He shouldn't be so mean to me. I *am* trying to be nice like father asked, but he makes it difficult."

The animosity between the duke and Seraphina had existed when Agatha had come to live with her. Bas's friendships had been fully in place before she ever knew them. It went back to his days at Eton. Agatha hadn't been there the first time Seraphina had met Riverdale but something terrible had happened. She didn't explain it all to her but she knew enough to understand the pain that lived inside of her. "We all have scars," she said to Seraphina. "Some are visible, and others are burrowed so deep inside we feel them rubbing us raw daily. No one can see them, but that doesn't make them less real."

"I know," she said softly. "You have your own that you bare and you understand more than anyone."

Agatha's scars were plentiful, but she didn't share them with everyone. They were her deepest, darkest secret and she didn't trust that pain with anyone. It was too raw and she didn't trust many not to use that agony against her. "If you need to do something to let that angst out," she began. "I'll help you. What do you want to do?"

Slowly her lips tilted upward. "You're the best sister a girl could ever have."

If only they were sisters in truth… "I don't need compliments. I've already agreed to whatever scheme you're concocting."

"I know," she bristled. "But it still should be said." Seraphina sighed. "I was thinking that perhaps we could play a game of sorts."

Agatha narrowed her gaze. "What sort of game."

It couldn't be that simple. If it had something to

do with Riverdale it wouldn't be necessarily a game full of laughter either. Seraphina meant to get some sort of revenge, and she could be diabolical at times. It was a trait she'd inherited from her father.

"What do you think about a scavenger hunt?" She wiggled her eyebrows. "You can help me write the clues."

"That's it?" Agatha had to be missing something. How did this help get with whatever scheme she had formed in her mind? "A scavenger hunt?"

"Oh it isn't a simple scavenger hunt," she teased. "This one will be remembered for a very long time, and trust me, the gentleman won't be happy with it either."

Now that sounded more like her… "All right, then let's get started."

Seraphina grinned and they walked away from the sitting room. She explained it all as they strolled casually down the hall and toward the game room. That was where the festivities for that evening would begin…

Dinner had been an unusual affair. Roarke couldn't quite discern the why of it, but Seraphina had been in unusual high spirits. Agatha had been a little fidgety, and Eva kept glancing at them with open curiosity. What had they done?

He didn't know how he knew, he just did. They'd left too willingly earlier from the sitting room. That was so unlike Seraphina it was almost like a blow to the head—he couldn't find a clear thought after it. She'd been so livid with Riverdale. There wasn't a chance in hell she'd let that exchange go so lightly.

Whatever she'd done, it made her far too cheerful. Dinner was pleasant because of that, but he was waiting for it all to fall down around him. They were walking out of the dining room together. The ladies were to go to the sitting room and the gentleman would retire to the game room for billiards. He did hope Riverdale would teach him that new move, but it could wait if Somerset wished to play first.

He leaned down and whispered to Agatha, who was walking next to him, "What did Seraphina do?"

She tilted her head to the side. "I don't know what you mean." She didn't meet his gaze as she spoke. Agatha was definitely hiding something.

"You're lying," he said in an easy tone. "But that's all right. I'll figure it out."

She laughed lightly. It sent shivers down his spine in warning. "You're right," she said. "It hasn't escaped my notice how clever you are. I'm sure you will discern the truth easily, and quickly at that."

Now he was worried. She seemed almost as gleeful as Seraphina had been at dinner. "I'm going to regret this aren't I?"

Agatha shrugged. "I wouldn't know, my lord. Do you think you have a reason to worry?" They reached the sitting room. She stopped and smiled at him. "Thank you for the escort my lord. Enjoy the rest of your evening." She curtsied and then left him alone in the hallway.

He shook his head several times. She was like a strong glass of the whiskey the Duke of Wharton preferred. It burned as it slid down his throat and left his head feeling muddled afterward.

"You look confused," Riverdale said. "What did she say to you?"

"It's what she didn't say that has me worried," he answered.

Riverdale frowned. "I have the same odd feeling." He shrugged. "I suppose we'll find out when they're ready to show their hand. Let's go play that game of billiards."

Somerset came over to join them. He laughed. "I can't wait to trounce the two of you. I've been practicing."

"Keep dreaming," Huntington drawled. "You'll never win."

They headed to the game room. The candles had already been lit in preparation, and a fire was in the hearth. Somerset had ordered the servants to prepare everything for their after dinner game. Huntington strolled over to the table to set up the game and froze. "Where are the balls?"

Somerset frowned. "They should be on the table. That is where we left them after our last game." They started to search the room but they couldn't find them anywhere. They couldn't very well play billiards without the bloody balls.

Roarke went over to the wall where the rack was for the cue sticks. "Um…" He shook his head. "That's not all that is missing" He pulled a sheet of paper out and brought it over to them.

"What is this?" Riverdale asked and took the paper from him. He unfolded it and cursed. "I'll strangle her."

"What?" Somerset said and took it from him.

He sighed and shook his head. "What did you do?" he asked Riverdale.

"Me?" He nearly bellowed the word. "That harridan is responsible for this. I didn't hide the damn billiard balls and decide to create a scavenger hunt out of them."

"She's not going to show us where they are," Roarke said in a calm tone. "If we want to find them, then we have to follow her clues."

Though after reading that note he wasn't so certain she had done it all on her own. That clue had a touch of Agatha in it. The two of them together could be quite devious. It was Riverdale's fault. He *had* started it with Seraphina earlier.

He glanced at the note again.

> It is time for a little fun. Follow the clues on this hunt to find all the balls and cues until it's done. This is your first clue: I have all your favorite things to read, get one from my collection and learn something new.

"I think I know where the first place is we have to go," Roarke said. It was probably the easiest clue they would encounter, but perhaps not. He under-stood it because of his encounter with Agatha earlier that day. He'd goaded her too.

"Where are we off to?" Somerset asked, resigned to his fate.

Riverdale was still steaming. "Tell us," he demanded.

"The library," he said in a calm tone.

They all left the game room and went to the library. There on the desk was the stack of books. One of the balls was on the desk next to that stack. "Where is the other clue?"

"It says to learn something new," Somerset said. "It's probably in one of the books."

"As in one of the books on this desk, or one in this library," Riverdale asked, a horrified expression on his face. There were a lot of books in the library and going through them all would take all night.

"I don't think they'd make it this hard so soon…" Roarke said. He picked up the book Agatha had been reading. It made sense to him it would be in there, but he could be wrong. He flipped through it until it stopped on a page outlining a safari. What did she hope he'd learn from this? "I found it," he said.

How profound, you've located clue two: I am always

running but I never walk. One of my hands is longer than the other and my numbers range from one to twelve.

This one was too easy… "It's a clock," he said.

"But what clock?" Somerset groaned. "There is a large clock in every major room of the house."

"Then we should get started," Roarke said. "I doubt it is in this one." He pointed to the clock against the far wall, but we can cross it off first."

Riverdale went over and opened the door leading to the insides that kept the clocks wound and running. There was no ball inside. "I am going to make sure she never does something like this ever again," he growled out the words.

"I understand you're frustrated," Roarke said. "But that won't help anyone."

"He's right," Somerset told him. "Let's finish this, and maybe when we're done we will still have time for a game."

Huntington didn't look as if he wanted to play any sort of game. If they left him alone he might go search for Seraphina and wring her neck. Roarke was actually having fun with the game they had set up. The women were clever indeed. Tomorrow he would search for Agatha and tell her as much. If Riverdale hoped to discourage Seraphina he should do the same…

It hadn't taken as long as Riverdale had feared to go through all the clues, but at the end of it none of them actually did want to play billiards. They retired for the evening, exhausted, but in good spirits. Even Riverdale had calmed down by the end. He would never admit it but he'd enjoyed himself.

Roarke had too, and he couldn't wait until he next saw Agatha… She wanted to play games? So be it. He would give her exactly what she wanted, and it would be more than she ever imagined it to be.

Five

After Agatha and Seraphina had finished hiding all the balls and sticks, creating the clues had been deliciously fun. Agatha couldn't recall the last time she had laughed so hard, or for so long. The gentlemen they'd hid the billiard balls, and cue sticks from probably didn't think it was as wonderful as she had, but that didn't matter. It was meant to be fun, and it had been.

They would get over whatever anger they felt upon finding the items missing, and losing their ability to play billiards immediately. They needed something to shake them up a bit. Riverdale had been acting like a complete arse and deserved to have to work for his moments of entertainment.

In short, Agatha couldn't be happier, and

Seraphina was overjoyed. Only one thing could have made it better—if they could have watched more closely as they fumbled through their clues. They had both decided that it would be better to be scarce as they searched. Riverdale's anger alone would be something they should avoid at all costs. He'd lash out and then an all out argument would ensue. Seraphina wouldn't have been able to keep her own temper in check.

All the excitement should have passed, and the three gentlemen should be in the game room now finally playing their game of billiards. Agatha had decided to leave her bedchamber and go to the library. She had already gone through the book she'd taken with her earlier, and was desperately in need of a new one to read. She did her best to remain as quiet as possible as she sneaked down the stairs. No one was around but that didn't stop her heart from rabidly beating with each step she took.

She kept searching everywhere as she went down the hall. Still nothing. Agatha wouldn't breathe easier until she reached the library and snatched another book off of the desk. Once inside the room she rushed over to the desk and frowned. Where were all her books? Fear seized her heart. She should have considered this. They had put one of the clues in the books, and that would have given them the opportunity to take them. Bas wouldn't have done it. Riverdale would have gladly taken part, but this couldn't have been his idea.

Only one of them had previously taken a book…

Agatha nibbled on her bottom lip. Should she go in search of Huntington? The first time he hadn't known how much it would distress her. Now though? He knew, and still he'd taken them. Was he that upset over the scavenger hunt? She honestly hadn't thought… She *hadn't* thought. If she had stopped to consider everything she would have been able to discern this possible outcome. In the moment she'd only wanted to help Seraphina, and it had been so much fun. The consequences were horrid though.

Where would he have gone? The sitting room as he had before? Probably not, but she had to start somewhere. Agatha sighed and left the library. It didn't take her long to reach the room. It was shrouded in darkness. If he was inside she couldn't see him. She considered leaving, but she couldn't without checking the room thoroughly. Agatha stepped inside and as soon as she reached the middle of the room the door slammed shut behind her.

She jumped and screamed. Her breathing became ragged as she rushed over to the door. The knob wouldn't turn, and the dratted thing wouldn't budge. She pulled on the door and started to bang on it. The darkness overwhelmed her and she sobbed uncontrollably.

No, no, no, no, no…

"Let me out," she said, her voice shook as she spoke. Her words were spoken frantically over and over again. Still the door didn't open.

"Agatha?" a man said. His tone sounded almost…sleepy.

She spun around at the sound of her name. "Who's there?"

"What's going on?" he asked.

When she had first come into the room she hadn't noticed anyone inside, but it had been so dark. He clearly hadn't heard her either, or had pretended that he hadn't. She knew who it was without him identifying himself. The second time he spoke she recognized his voice. "Huntington," she said his name. Her voice was barely above a whisper and her anxiety still reverberated through it.

"Yes," he said. Huntington sounded closer than before. "Why is the door closed?"

"Someone shut it," she said. *Drat*. Why couldn't she get her voice under control?

"Then open it," he said. "There's no reason to stay inside the room."

As if she hadn't tried that. She rolled her eyes even though he couldn't see her. "If you think you can open it then by all means, give it a go."

He slid past her and turned the knob. It didn't move. Huntington yanked on the door and then lost his grip, and fell on his arse. She lifted her hand to her lips to restrain the laughter that bubbled to the surface. "Well?" Agatha lifted a brow. "Stand up now. Open it. I don't have all night." Perhaps she was being a bit shrewish, but she couldn't help herself. He'd been so bloody arrogant and deserved a little distain.

"It's stuck," he said belligerently.

"It is?" She feigned innocence. "Why, how could I have possibly missed that?"

Her eyes were starting to adjust to the dark. Huntington turned his head toward her but she still could not make out his features. He sighed. "Sarcasm will not aid us in exiting this room," he said in a calm tone. "Who would have locked us inside?"

"How would I know?" she said mulishly.

"I didn't expect you would," he told her. "I was speaking aloud. It helps me to think."

Agatha moved past him and found her way to the settee. She didn't know how they would get out of the room, and she was suddenly fatigued. She'd let him sit on the floor and stare at the door. Maybe he'd have some luck where she'd failed…

ROARKE CURSED UNDER HIS BREATH. HOW THE HELL had this happened? He had come into the sitting room for a bit of peace and quiet. Riverdale had been in a fit after that scavenger hunt and Roarke wanted some time to think. He'd wanted to plan something to get Agatha's attention—but this… She'd been hysterical earlier. Her shrieks had shocked his senses and he'd come awake quite suddenly.

Was this Riverdale's doing?

He didn't think either of his friends would lock him in a room with Agatha, but he couldn't think of who would have. Agatha seemed calmer. She'd snapped at him and had leaned on some sarcasm, but he didn't think she was all right. He should ask her. Her panicked screeching had been disturbing. "I don't know how long we will be stuck in here," he told her.

"You don't think the door is going to budge then?" Her tone was even, but it still seemed off.

"No," he said in a soft tone. "I'm afraid you're going to have to put up with my company. At least until morning…." This room was used often enough during the day someone would open that door. "A maid is likely to open it to clean it then."

"Did you take my books?" she asked.

That startled him. "Your books?" Did she mean that stack of traveling guides on Bas's desk in the library? "Why would I take them?"

"You took that one…" She sighed. "They're all gone. I thought perhaps you took them because of that."

He shook his head, but then thought perhaps she couldn't see him. There were no candles in the room or he'd light one. He had noticed the lack of a candelabrum when he first entered the room, but since he didn't need any light that hadn't bothered him. The lack of fire in the hearth might be an issue though. The room might catch a chill overnight. "I wouldn't take your books," he said softly. "I made that mistake once and I have no wish to upset you." Play with her a little bit, yes, but hurt her no. Taking her books would distress her. "Why were you upset earlier? Was it the missing books?"

"The books' disappearance did upset me," she told him. "But to the extreme I'd cry over them. I'd get mad first."

"You don't like being locked in," he guessed. What had happened to her to make her fear that? No one reacted as violently as she had without reason.

"My father used to lock me in my bedroom," she said almost absentmindedly. As if speaking about it was so distressing that she had to distance herself from the truth. "Sometimes in a closet…"

His heart lurched. He wanted to pull her into his arms and comfort her. How could anyone be that cold-hearted and to his own daughter… "I'm sorry," he said. A lump had formed in his throat and he found it difficult to swallow.

"Why?" she said. "You didn't do it to me."

"That doesn't mean I can't feel something for you," he told her. "He caused you pain and you relived it earlier. I'd take that pain away if I could." And if her father weren't already dead he'd wring his neck for her…

"You can't erase my past." Her tone was firm

and it sounded as if she was more herself. "It's part of who I am, and if not for that I might not be the same person."

"I suppose that is true," he conceded. That didn't mean that he would stop hurting for her. "Everything we encounter impacts our life in some way. It's part of life."

"Yes," she agreed. "Why are you in here?"

Agatha wanted to move on to a different topic. He'd allow it because this one was probably too painful for her. "I came in here to think," he answered honestly. "I wanted to come up with a fun game for you and Seraphina to play as you did for us."

"Did you enjoy the scavenger hunt then?" She sounded a little pleased. Roarke wanted to join her on the settee but didn't think it a wise action.

"Bas and I found it quite amusing," he told her. "Riverdale…" He laughed softly. "Seraphina might want to avoid him for the rest of the house party."

"That's not likely to happen," Agatha said. Amusement filled her voice as she spoke. "Eva has plans, and it would hurt her if we hid in our rooms the entire time."

"There is that," he agreed. "Riverdale will have to control that temper of his then."

"Did you think of something?" she asked. "A game that is?"

He hadn't. Nothing that he could actually engage her in anyway... His thoughts had drifted to a different sort of diversion. One filled with heat, pleasure, and they would both be naked. A bed would be preferable, but any soft surface would do. He'd fallen asleep dreaming of hot kisses and soft moans. "What sort of games do you like?"

"I'm not much of a game person. Seraphina has to convince me to participate in them." She sighed. "I prefer books and solitude."

He could see how she might. Agatha had spent the first part of her life alone, and now being around others must distress her. "That's too bad," he said. "I thought we could spend this time doing something more enjoyable, but if you don't like to play I won't make you."

She was quiet for several moments. "What did you have in mind?"

He had her. Now that he'd caught her attention what should he suggest? An image of those kisses crossed his mind. "We can't do much in the dark," he said. "We could tell each other stories."

"Like how Eva read that book to Bas last year at Christmas?" Agatha said.

"I suppose it is similar," he said. "But the difference is we have to create our own stories."

"I'm not that creative," she told him.

Roarke doubted that was true. "You didn't help with those clues on the scavenger hunt?"

"I did…" She blew out a breath. "That's not the same though and you know it."

"Fine," he said. "Then what should we do?" How about a kiss? Should he suggest that?

Agatha shivered. It was already starting to grow colder in the room. Roarke leapt to his feet and strolled across to her. He sat down next to her. "Will you allow me to hold you?"

"Why?" She sounded a little panicked.

"You're cold," he said softly. "The only heat I can offer is from my own body." His voice was a little hoarse. He might come to regret this…"Let me help you, Agatha."

She didn't say a word. He waited patiently for her to agree. After a few painful moments of waiting finally she said, "Yes." She moved toward him. "Hold me."

Roarke wrapped his arms around her and pulled her onto his lap. He closed his eyes and just enjoyed the moment. She felt so good in his arms and her scent…it was divine. Like lavender and vanilla, and all things right in the world. He would not take advantage of her. She trusted him, and he would not abuse the faith she'd put in him.

One day he would kiss her though, but not when she felt trapped and afraid. She leaned her head on his shoulder and he nearly groaned. It was going to be one hell of a long night…

Six

Warmth spread through Agatha and she snuggled closer to bask in it a little longer. She couldn't remember the last time she'd felt so wonderful and safe. Nothing could tear her away from this wonderful place. She wanted to stay where she was, forever, if at all possible.

She sat up suddenly, remembering exactly where she was, and the man's arms that had been wrapped around her so snuggly. "Sssh," he said softly. "You're safe."

Agatha pulled away from him and scooted over to the other side of the settee. She shouldn't have allowed herself to be held by him. It was dangerous to her heart and her reputation. It was still dark in the room, but she could still see some of her surroundings. With the loss of Huntington's warmth Agatha shivered.

"You should come back over here," he said, and patted the seat next to him. "You're cold."

"No," she said. "It's not…" Agatha couldn't find the right word. Safe didn't fit… He would never hurt her, but she still didn't feel right with the idea of being so close to him. "I'd just rather not." That was the best her overwhelmed mind could come up with.

Huntington chuckled. "I won't argue with you. I've learned it is futile when you've decided upon something."

"I didn't realize you paid me that much mind," she said solemnly. They had interacted a lot over the past several years, but she didn't think he paid her much attention. Her feelings for him were irrelevant. The marquess clearly didn't notice her as anything more than the duke's ward. Or so she'd believed… What if she had been wrong? No, she couldn't have read the situation incorrectly. Huntington didn't have any feelings for her. At least not the sort she hoped he might.

"You and Seraphina are a matched pair in

many aspects," he told her. "You're just quieter than she is."

That was true. Agatha didn't like when anyone actually noticed her. When they did their loud whispers started, along with the speculation about the duke and her parentage. She hated that they believed he was actually her father. The Duke of Wharton hadn't taken her in because she was his bastard daughter, but she didn't feel the need to explain that to any of the ton. "Seraphina doesn't suffer fools."

"And neither do you," he said. There was a bit of humor in his tone. "But your revenge isn't as easily traced."

"I don't need credit for my good deeds." Her lips twitched as she fought a smile. "The reward is in the knowing."

"That's what I like about you," he explained. "Your altruistic heart."

Agatha couldn't hold in the laughter any longer. It spilled out of her and filled the room. "You didn't have to make it sound as if I don't do anything good."

"Oh," he began. "But you do. Even when you're bad, your good."

She sighed. Agatha wasn't sure what he meant to do with this line of conversation. Did he hope to take her mind off of their circumstances? Was he being truly honest with her? This was all new to her and she felt out of place. It felt so easy and natural, but she couldn't rely on her own instincts. She wanted him too much to trust herself where he was concerned. "I'm never bad," she said in a haughty tone.

He laughed. "Right. *Never.*" Huntington winked.

"Should we try the door again?" she asked. Surely they wouldn't be locked in there the entire night.

"I can if you wish," he said. "But it is unlikely that it is magically unlocked. Servants should be waking soon, and when one comes to clean in here we can make our escape then."

That wouldn't work at all… If a servant found them together it would be disastrous. "That can't happen." Her voice took on a shrill tone. She shot to her feet and paced in front of the settee. "I'll be ruined."

Huntington stood and stepped in front of her path. He placed his hands on her arms and held her still. "Agatha," he said softly. "Calm down. It will be all right."

"How can you be so certain?" Her heart

thudded heavily in her chest. Agatha wanted him more than anything that she'd ever wanted in her life. Even when her father kept her locked in her room and she prayed for her freedom—that didn't compare to what she felt for Huntington. What she didn't want was for him to be forced into something he didn't want as well. She wanted him to be happy. That didn't include the possibility of a marriage to her that he didn't actually desire.

"Somerset wouldn't hire servants that gossiped where they shouldn't," Huntington explained. "Or have you forgotten his skills as a spy?"

Agatha frowned. She had forgotten that fact. In her overexcitement about her current situation she hadn't taken any of that into account. Sebastian had stopped working for the Duke of Wharton in that capacity, but he wouldn't have lost those skills he'd learned. "You're right," she conceded.

"Of course I am," he said in a soothing tone. "I always am."

"And so modest too," she said in an apathetic tone.

"Darling," he said a little wickedly. "Modesty is for those that don't know exactly what they have to offer. I'm too skilled to allow the world to believe differently."

Was it any wonder why she adored this man? That didn't mean she could let him become too complacent and address her with impertinent endearments. "I'm not your darling."

"Aren't you?" he said softly. This was far too intimate…

Agatha suddenly remembered that his hands were on her arms and they were close. Very, very close. All she had to do was take one step forward and he could hold her against him. If she allowed it…they could do much, much more than that. Did she dare?

"No," she said. Her tone was barely above a whisper. "I belong to no one." That wasn't true. She'd given him her heart years ago, but she'd never told him, and she never planned to either.

ROARKE COULD JUST MAKE OUT HER FACE IN THE low light. She might have said she wasn't his, but he didn't believe her. He shouldn't push her to admit what they both knew, but he was tired of fighting his own feelings. She had to stop doing the same.

"Of course you don't," he told her. "You wouldn't be you if you were in someone else's shadow." He lifted his hand and caressed her cheek. "You're perfect."

"I'm not," she disagreed.

She didn't see what he did. There was no other woman like her. He couldn't imagine a world without her in it. Roarke should have told her what she meant to him a long time ago. He had been fighting himself and his stupid beliefs for so long. She was too good for him. "That will be one of the things I'm certain we will disagree on over the years."

"What do you mean?"

"I'm sure we will have ample opportunity to argue about many different topics." He stroked her hair. It was so soft. She was so utterly lovely. "I believe I do look forward to it."

"You're tone is odd…" She frowned. "What is going on inside that head of yours?"

"Did you know you're standing under the mistletoe again?" he asked her. She glanced up and stared at the foliage that had been pinned above the settee.

"Did they move it?" Agatha frowned. "Wasn't it in the doorway before?"

"I don't recall," he answered. Honestly he didn't really care either. He was grateful for the mistletoe.

It gave him an excuse to do what he wanted to do anyway. "Does it matter?"

"I don't suppose it does." She nibbled on her bottom lip. His gaze trailed over the press of her teeth on her plump lip. "Eva has taken these decorations far too seriously."

"I don't know," he said. "I rather like what she's done so far."

Agatha's gaze met his. She inhaled sharply. Oh, yes, she knew. He didn't hold back his desire for her. It had been blazing inside of him for too long now. She wasn't afraid of being trapped in the room any longer. Instead outrage had filled her and it had given her something to latch onto. He could use that to his advantage. Roarke could kiss her and not feel guilty for taking the time to feel a brief moment of pleasure.

"Huntington…"

"Roarke," he corrected. "To you I'm Roarke, and you, my dear, are my Agatha." He leaned down until his lips were near hers. They weren't touching yet. He wanted her to feel the anticipation, the need, and all the desire he had simmering beneath the surface. Roarke wanted her as hot as he was, and he prayed that this wouldn't be a mistake.

Her mouth opened and her breathing was shallow. Roarke leaned down and lightly grazed her lips with his. A soft awakening, an acceptance, and a capitulation… He didn't need any more signs. She leaned into him and he pulled her closer, wrapping his arms around her. Then he pressed his lips to hers once again and deepened the kiss. Her moans filled the room and every inch of him filled with desire. For her, and only her… Roarke would never want another woman the way he did her.

He slid his hand down her back. Roarke wanted to strip her bare and make love to her. He couldn't let it go that far though. She would regret it, and he never wanted her to have any reason to doubt what he felt for her. Everything between them had to be done the right way. Which meant, as much as he would like to continue to kiss her, he had to stop.

It killed something inside of him, but he lifted his head and stopped kissing her. Her eyelids had fluttered shut. She opened her eyes slowly and met his gaze. Agatha looked a little dazed. Her lips were even plumper than they had been before. Roarke wanted to give in and kiss her again. Bloody hell… He had to get control of himself.

"Why did you stop?" Agatha asked in a breath-less tone.

Roarke groaned. "Because you're too tempting."

She smiled. "I am?" Agatha moved closer and rubbed her hand over his chest. "Clearly I'm not that much of a temptation. You have no trouble resisting me."

Roarke cursed and pulled her back into his arms. "God help me," he muttered under his breath, then kissed her again. She tasted so good, and he couldn't get enough of her.

Agatha lifted her hands and tugged on his hair, pulling him closer to her. Their shared passion exploded around them. Nothing mattered but what they felt for each other and finding some way to get closer. He needed to feel her skin against his.

He cupped her breast in his hand. She moaned when he slipped his hand inside her bodice and rubbed his thumb over her nipple. It was the sweetest sound he'd ever heard. Roarke leaned down and trailed kisses over her neck and down her chest. He wanted to kiss every inch of her.

"Please," Agatha begged. "I need more."

He wanted to give her everything she needed. Roarke couldn't do this to her though. She had been afraid she would be ruined before. If they kept going her reputation would be in tatters. He had to stop before it was too late. She didn't deserve to be the subject of gossip of any kind. "Darling," he said. His voice was hoarse from barely contained desire. "We have to take a step back."

"No," she said. "I want you to kiss me again."

"What is going on in here?" a man demanded.

They had both been so engrossed in each other they hadn't heard the door open behind them. Roarke turned toward the person who had spoken and groaned. That was the last person he wanted to find them. "Hello, Your Grace," he said in as calm of a tone as he could manage.

The Duke of Wharton was staring at the two of them. Almost as if he had planned to find them in a compromising situation… Perhaps he had and had been waiting to walk in. Roarke planned on asking him a few questions, but first, he had other priorities. He had to protect Agatha and he would do anything to do that.

Seven

Agatha was speechless. Her mind had so much racing through it she couldn't form a straight thought. His kisses… They'd made her a little woozy and perhaps drunk on… What? Passion? That had to be it, but she had no experience with being either inebriated or experiencing passion. This was all new to her, and now she had to think properly and couldn't. The duke looked most displeased and she had nothing to offer to him in explanation. It didn't matter that they'd been locked in the room together for hours. They should have resisted temptation.

Still, she had no regrets. Agatha would not apologize for giving in and enjoying Roarke's kisses. He'd given her permission to use his given name, and she refused to think of him as Huntington or the marquess ever again. He'd be Roarke to her forever now. There was no going back even if she wanted to, and she most certainly didn't want to.

Agatha swallowed hard. "Your Grace," she said, and then curtsied. It was amazing she managed to say that much. Hopefully he didn't demand an extensive explanation. There was no way she would be able to do more than stammer a few words together.

"I'm waiting," the duke said. He glanced from Roarke and then to Agatha expectantly. "What did I just walk in on."

"Why are you here?" Roarke asked. Was he avoiding answering the question? Not that Agatha could really blame him. She didn't want to admit to anything either, and she wasn't the least bit ashamed by her actions.

The duke narrowed his gaze. "Why doesn't matter boy. Answer me."

Agatha's lips twitched. Roarke didn't like being referred to as a boy. His lips had formed a straight line as if he fought the urge to correct the duke. "It seems as if you have already made up your mind. Why should I try to explain anything?"

Oh, that wasn't good at all. If he had any hope

of avoiding marriage to her he had to do better than that. The duke would insist on a betrothal now. Agatha had to say something. "It's the mistletoe you see." That sounded ridiculous.

"The mistletoe?" The duke raised a brow. "What are you sputtering on about?"

Agatha pointed toward the ceiling. "The mistletoe." As if that were explanation enough. "It's…you know."

Roarke chuckled under his breath. "I'm not sure he does love. Why don't you explain it a little better for him."

She glared at him. Damn him. Why wasn't he helping her? She wanted to smack that smug smile off of his face. "None of it meant anything you see. It was all the mistletoe. Really Eva shouldn't hang so much of it up."

Agatha hoped her friend would forgive her for blaming the mistletoe and her actions on her decorations. Though she did think Roarke used them as permission to kiss her. He might not have otherwise.

"I'm not so certain the duke believes you," Roarke said. His tone suggested he wasn't about to deny anything either. He'd decided on something and was not intractable. He could be so darned stubborn at times.

"I do not," the duke agreed. "It's clear you're compromised dear."

"Thoroughly," Roarke agreed.

Why did he sound so happy with that turn of events? What the blazes was wrong with him? Did he want to be forced to marry her? She would love for him to ask for her hand. Agatha had loved him for so long… She didn't want him to have to marry her though. A marriage like that was…well not a marriage she had ever wanted for herself. Whatever passion they felt for each other would be fleeting, and when that fizzled out what would they have left between them?

The duke met Roarke's gaze. He was quiet for several stifling minutes. "What are you going to do about it?"

Roarke grinned. "I would think that would be obvious."

Agatha stared at the two of them as if they had lost their damned minds. They were discussing this as if she wasn't even in the room. This could not be happening. The entire night was one disaster after another. Why had he kissed her? Did he not realize that it could lead to this very situation? She had to find some way to prevent what was about to happen. "I don't think anything is quite so evident," she said in a mulish tone. "Before the two of you think you can decide my future for me don't you think you should consult me?"

"You did all the deciding on your own already," the duke said. "When you allowed him to have liberties he never should have taken in the first place."

She lifted a brow. "He didn't go that far." She lifted her chin defiantly. "No one has to know what happened here. It can remain quiet as long as—" She gestured between the duke and Roarke. "—the two of you don't go spreading tales like two gossiping matrons."

"It's not that simple," the duke said.

"Isn't it though?" She was not going to let them convince her she *had* to marry Roarke. It didn't matter that she *wanted* to. He didn't and that was all that mattered. "Please explain the parts that are too complicated for my female mind to understand."

The duke sighed. "He took liberties…"

"And?" Agatha interrupted. "That means I'm not tainted by his touch. It doesn't matter that he hasn't taken my innocence. He kissed me and touched me so now I'm not worthy of an unmarried state or even a different man to say vows with?"

She wanted to hit something. "The standards a woman has to maintain is ridiculous."

"And yet there is nothing we can do to change them," the duke told her.

"That's not true," she said. "You could do something to change them. And by you, I mean men, but none of you will. All men think they know what is best for us females and are not likely to change their mind anytime soon." She sighed. "I had hoped you were more enlightened." She met the duke's gaze as she spoke. "But I see I am wrong."

They were going to decide for her on this and didn't think she should worry her pretty little head about it. Agatha had never wanted to give in to the urge to throw a temper tantrum more.

ROARKE HAD TO DO SOMETHING OR THIS SITUATION would only get worse. He had a feeling that Agatha's main objection had nothing to do with the actual marriage part of this impending bargain. Her doubts had everything to do with him and what he felt for her. She probably didn't realize how he felt about her. He wasn't certain of her feelings for him either, but he could guess. Roarke hoped she felt the same as he did, but they hadn't talked about any of that. There was a lot they hadn't discussed and should.

He faced the duke. "Can you give us some time alone?"

"I don't think I should," the duke told him. "You two seem to land into nothing but trouble when you are left to do as you wish."

Roarke couldn't fault the duke for thinking that. He had walked in on them in each other's arms. "Perhaps you can concentrate on why we were locked in here together. We didn't spend all this time together by choice."

"Is that so?" The duke frowned. "Someone intentionally locked you in this room. Who would do that?"

He shrugged. "I wouldn't presume to make a guess." He didn't look at Agatha as he spoke. "I, uh, fell asleep in here. When I woke Agatha was pounding on the door." Roarke didn't need to explain anything else. The duke stiffened at his words. If anyone was aware of Agatha's fears it was the duke. He'd taken her in as his ward when she was still young.

The duke turned toward Agatha. "Do you know who did it?"

She shook her head. "It was too dark. I thought I was alone." Agatha shrugged slightly. "I went looking for my books to look over. I couldn't sleep."

"The books Sebastian had set aside for you?" the duke asked.

She nodded. "Yes," she told him. "They were missing again from the library. I thought perhaps Roa—the Marquess of Huntington borrowed them again. He had them in this room the last time they were no longer in the library."

Roarke held back a smile. She'd almost said his name. If she had the duke wouldn't doubt there was some more intimacy between them than she wanted him to believe. "I didn't take them this time." He wouldn't do that to her a second time. "Perhaps Riverdale has them. He wasn't pleased by the billiard equipment being used for a scavenger hunt."

Agatha's lips twitched. "That was Seraphina's grand plan."

"But you did help her," Roarke reminded Agatha. "Riverdale will probably focus his more nefarious ideas in her direction, but you won't be left alone in his schemes. He probably has your books—or Somerset has them for some reason. I doubt he'd keep them from you if he does have them."

The duke tilted his head to the side and stared at the two of them thoughtfully. "You have both given me much to consider." He turned toward Roarke. "What is Riverdale planning for my daughter? Should I be concerned."

Roarke shook his head. "No," he told the duke. "He would never harm her. She played a bit of a prank on him earlier because he upset her. He'll probably do something harmless but one she won't be able to miss either. I don't know that with any certainty, but I assume he will. They have been playing these sort of games with each other for a while now."

"I asked her to behave during this house party. Clearly she cannot follow simple instructions where the Duke of Riverdale is concerned." The duke sighed. "I'll have to talk to her about all of this too. I'm not happy with any of you."

Roarke would not apologize for kissing Agatha. He had wanted her and still did. "My apologies for disappointing you." He wouldn't say more than that.

"If we are done discussing this at length I'm still tired. I'd like to return to my chamber and try to get some sleep." Agatha yawned. Roarke wanted to follow her up to her bedchamber and kiss her again. He'd like it even more if he could follow her inside and love her all night long. Soon he hoped he'd have that privilege every day or night of the rest of their lives.

The duke faced her. "We have much more to discuss," he told her.

"Must we do it all tonight?" She said in a frustrated tone. "Nothing is going to be solved right this moment." Agatha glared at him, then turned it on Roarke.

"All right," the duke conceded. "But I will discuss this with you after I do some investigating. When I send for you I expect you to respond promptly."

She nodded. "Very well. May I be excused?"

"Yes," the duke said, then turned to Roarke. "But you stay."

Agatha left the room. Roarke wished the duke hadn't commanded him to stay. He might have followed Agatha. Though that might be why the duke had asked him to remain in the room. After Agatha was gone he turned toward the duke. "You don't need to dress me down. I know what is expected of me."

"That's not what I want to discuss with you," the duke told him. "That part can wait until tomorrow after we do some investigating. Someone wanted me to find the two of you like this. That is why none of this is as simple as Agatha wants to believe it to be."

Roarke frowned. "What do you mean?"

"The two of you were locked in this room on purpose." The duke stared at him. "That means there is another person involved. Someone we don't know, is very much aware you compromised Agatha. They might not be aware of what the two of you did while you were alone, but that doesn't really matter does it?"

Roarke shook his head and cursed. "We need to find out who is playing games that aren't as innocent as they seem."

The duke nodded. "And for us to uncover it I'll need you help and my nephew's. He isn't going to like it but he has to come out of retirement." The Earl of Somerset was one of the Duke of Wharton's personally trained spies. Something he stopped doing once he married.

"I'll speak to him," Roarke said.

"No," the duke said. "I will. I need you to do something else." He pulled a parchment out of the pocket of his waistcoat. "I want you to handle this." He handed it to Roarke.

He opened the missive and cursed again.

If you care about your ward's reputation you should go look in the sitting room now and save her from certain ruin.

The note wasn't signed. Who could have done this? "You didn't see who left this for you?"

He shook his head. "It was on the writing desk in my bedchamber. I didn't see it until moments before I came down here. I had trouble sleeping and decided to work."

"Then we have nothing to go on…"

"We can question the servants. Someone must know something," the duke said.

Roarke agreed. He didn't like any of this. Who wanted to ruin Agatha? This had to do with her more than him. They had referenced her in the note. "I'll start at first light. When I learn something I'll report back."

"Good," the duke said. "After we solve this little

mystery we can discuss your impending betrothal to my ward."

Roarke nodded. He had no issue with that plan. "Until we next speak." He put the missive in his pocket. Then left the duke alone in the room. There was much to do and dawdling with the duke wouldn't help him with his task.

Eight

Agatha sat in the sitting room and stared out the window. The mistletoe had moved again. Someone was having fun moving the blasted foliage around. It now hung directly in the middle of the room. She would have to avoid that area while it was there, and when she entered a room she would have to glance upward to see where more of the infernal plant was hanging. She did not want to be caught under any more mistletoe. It had been nothing but trouble for her.

"Are you hiding in here?" Seraphina asked from the entrance to the room. "I've been looking for you."

"You have?" Agatha glanced at her. "Is there a particular reason you needed to find me?" She wasn't certain she wanted to become embroiled in another of Seraphina's schemes. The last one may have had abysmal repercussions for her. That is if the Duke of Riverdale had taken her books… There was no proof, that she was aware of, that he had.

"Nothing specific…" Seraphina nibbled on her bottom lip. "I had hoped I could talk with you. I've just come from one of my father's lectures. He's most displeased with me."

Agatha wasn't surprised. "Was it terrible?" She had expected the duke would reprimand Seraphina for her actions. He didn't even have all the details, but that didn't really matter did it. The duke had asked one thing from his daughter—to not bicker or anything of the sort with the Duke of Riverdale. The trick she'd pulled on him regarding the billiard equipment had been much, much more than that. Their quarreling had been a catalyst to that little scheme of hers.

"No more than it usually is," Seraphina proclaimed before sitting down on a nearby chair and slumping down in it most unlady like. "He expects so much from me and I did try to do as he wished. But that man…" She opened and closed her hands as if she were about to throttle the Duke of Riverdale—and she may have tried if he were actually in the room with them. "He frustrates me so."

"I'm aware of how he affects you," Agatha said softly. Had the duke mentioned how he'd come by the knowledge of her little scheme? Would he have told Seraphina about what had happened between Agatha and Roarke? "Did the duke seem particularly agitated today?" He hadn't yet sent for her. She'd been waiting for him to do so for hours now. It was starting to make her especially nervous.

"No," Seraphina said. "But it is always hard to tell with him. He keeps his feelings properly contained—as he expects me to do."

That sounded like the duke. He expected both Agatha and Seraphina to remain in control of their emotions—especially the ones that might lead to a scandal. He didn't let anyone know what he was thinking let alone what he might feel. "Is that difficult for you?" Her own father had never been one to hold back what he thought or felt. Agatha had always been a disappointment to him.

She shrugged. "It used to be," she admitted. "But I know he cares about me and only wants to protect me. He'd never hurt me or do anything that might harm me. I can endure his occasional disapproval."

"He is a good man," Agatha said—more to herself than to Seraphina. Perhaps she shouldn't be so difficult. When he finally asked to speak to her she would at least listen to what he had to say. Besides, she had willingly kissed Roarke. It wasn't the duke's fault she fell prey to the marquess's charms and stupidly fell in love with the dratted man. The duke had made sure to look after her ever since he'd come for her several years earlier. He protected her. Nothing about that had changed.

"He'll want to talk with you next," Seraphina warned her. "Someone told him about the scavenger hunt we arranged for Sebastian and his cohorts." She wrinkled her nose. "I don't think Riverdale would have run to him and complained. Who do you think did it?"

Should she tell her? What kind of interrogation would that open up for her if she did? Agatha sighed. "The Marquess of Huntington," she told her.

"He did?" Seraphina frowned. "How do you know?" She sat up straighter and narrowed her gaze. "What are you hiding?"

More than Agatha wished to impart… Luckily

or perhaps unluckily she didn't have to answer Seraphina. A footman came in the room before she had a chance to speak. "Miss Agatha," he said. "The Duke of Wharton asked me to give you this." He handed her a note, then left.

"It's your turn isn't it?" Seraphina said as Agatha read over the note.

"It is," she said in a quiet tone. Seraphina assumed Agatha would get the same lecture she had. Hers would be far worse. She would have to listen to him convince her marrying Roarke was in her best interest, and she would then have to refuse his good advice. She would not marry a man that didn't love her. Desire wasn't enough to base a marriage on. "I best go to him or he'll be upset I dawdled."

"Good luck," Seraphina said. "You'll need it."

More than she knew…

Agatha left the sitting room and went to where the duke had set up to work while he was in residence. It was a small study that the estate manager used when he was there. He had gone to spend time with his family for the Christmastide season and that left the room unoccupied for a few weeks.

She knocked on the door. "Your Grace," she said.

The duke glanced up from his desk and motioned for her to come inside. She strolled in and sat in a nearby chair and waited. He would speak when he was ready to and not a moment before. After several moments he glanced up at her. "There are several things we need to discuss," he said.

"There is?" She furrowed her brows. Agatha had assumed there would be only one thing the duke wanted to discuss with her. "What should we start with first?"

He sighed. "First there is this." He picked up a book and handed it to her. "I believe this is the one you have been reading. The others are back in the library."

She took the book and frowned. "Where was it?"

"In the library," he said. "Whoever took it had already put it back when we went searching. I spoke to Riverdale and he never touched the books and insists, while he was irritated about the scavenger hunt, he hadn't planned any sort of retribution." His lips went upward slightly as he fought a smile. "That doesn't mean that he wouldn't have if I hadn't taken a moment to speak with him. He was most frustrated with my daughter."

"He often is." All Seraphina had to do was

breathe and he was irritated with her. "At least the books were returned." She wasn't so enamored with them now though. There were far bigger concerns she had to contend with.

"Yes," he said. The duke leaned back in his chair. "Do you remember the day I came and asked you if you would like to come live with me?"

It was a day she would never forget. "I do." Where was he going with this?

"Do you remember what I said to you about times a person must be more circumspect?" he asked in a soft tone. "And if you knew the difference between those times."

"You said that you expected me to be myself," she said. "And I have. I don't expect I'll change now. It's far too late for that."

"I don't presume you'll change and I'd never ask that of you," he said. "I don't want you to be anyone other than you are." He smiled as he met her gaze. "You are so much like your mother sometimes it hurts to look at you."

Agatha's heart was in her throat. He never spoke of her mother. All he'd ever said was she'd been important to him. Should she ask? Many people gossiped about her true relationship with the duke and why he'd taken her in all those years ago. They assumed he was her true father and that was why the baron had treated her so poorly. "Why was my mother important to you. Can you tell me about her?" She knew very little about her mother and was desperate to know more.

He tapped his fingers on the mahogany desk and didn't speak for several moments. His green eyes, so much like her own, was a little misty. "My father wasn't—how should I say this." He closed his eyes and took a fortifying breath. "He wasn't faithful to my mother."

"Many men are that way in the ton," Agatha said. "It's one of the reasons I do not believe in marriage."

He frowned at her. "I can't dispute that but we will discuss that in a few moments. You asked about your mother…" He shook his head slightly. "I didn't know about her until after she married your father—about six months after my father died. It had taken me that long to rifle through the mess he'd made of the estates."

"What did you find?" she asked in a soft tone.

"As I said, my father had mistresses—many of them. More than I ever wished to know about. Somehow, by some miracle, he didn't sire a plethora of bastards." He sighed heavily. "Except one. Your mother was the result of an affair he'd had with a married woman. He didn't have to support her, but he had wanted to leave her a token. A necklace that had belonged to his mother—it took me a while to find her."

"Did you give it to her?" Agatha asked. If he had she'd never seen it.

He shook his head. "She asked me to hold on to it. Your mother didn't trust her husband not to sell it or take it from her. She was pregnant with you when I found her." He smiled. "All she asked from me was that if something happened to her that I look after her child, and when the time came, to give that necklace to them. I'll give it to you when we return to my estate" He paused briefly, then continued "I think she knew somehow she was going to die."

"Perhaps," she said. "Or maybe she saw the baron for the monster he was. Why did she marry him?"

"Her father, her legal one, didn't give her a choice. He knew she wasn't his and sold her to the first man that asked for her hand. He didn't care what happened to her." He met her gaze. "I won't do that to you. If you truly do not wish to marry the

Marquess of Huntington I won't force you to. But there are some things you should know."

She had already learned so much. The duke was her uncle, but no one would ever know that. It explained so much. What else could he possibly have to tell her? "Such as?"

"The man that inherited the baron's estate, your father's heir, paid someone to ruin you. Apparently you have a small inheritance that your father left you that you would only get if you didn't create any scandal by your twenty first birthday."

"And if I create a scandal?" she asked.

"Then it reverts back to the estate—which is hurting for funds at the moment. The new baron needs that money," the duke explained.

"Let me guess," she began. "He decided to arrange for me to ruin my reputation."

"In a manner of speaking. You and Huntington played right into his agent's hands. Sebastian recently hired a new footman. This man has been keeping tabs on everyone and he's the one that locked you in the sitting room, and he is also the one that arranged for me to find you there. No matter what, my dear, you are ruined."

That was what he meant when he said it wasn't that simple. "You think I should marry him don't you. I don't care if I get the baron's money. I'd rather not have it if I'm being honest."

"I understand," he said. "As I said—it is your decision, but I would like you to at least consider it. Not for the inheritance, but for yourself. Talk with the marquess before you make that decision and let me know what you decide. As far as to the inheritance—if you don't want it we can use it for something else. Perhaps a charitable fund of some sort."

Agatha did like that idea. "I'll consider it."

"Good," the duke said. "Go to the library. The marquess is waiting there for you."

Agatha sighed and then left the room. She would go talk with Roarke, but she would not promise to marry him. Without love she wouldn't have him. Even for funds to start her own charity of some sort.

Nine

Roarke sat on the settee in the library. He was exhausted and anxious at the same time. If he tried to sleep he wouldn't be able to—not that he wanted to. He had been up helping the duke and Sebastian uncover their little mystery for hours now. With the mystery solved he now had one thing left to accomplish—convince Agatha that marrying him was the answer to everything.

He didn't know if she would agree. Roarke prayed that she would, but he was no fool. This was a monumental task before him. She'd already started to dig in her heels and refuse before he'd had a chance to even ask her. He knew what she believed, and making her rethink that assumption would be nearly impossible.

Was the duke done speaking with her?

Hell, waiting was killing him. He wasn't known for his patience. Rushing in and worrying about the consequences later was what he usually did. Hence his current dilemma… He ran his fingers through his hair in frustration. Where was she?

The sun was starting to set. Soon he would have to light some candles to see her properly. Should he do so now to ensure there was light in the room? The fire was already blazing in the hearth so there wouldn't be a chill in the room. He was about to stand and look for something to light the candles and froze when Agatha entered the room.

His heart thundered inside his chest and the beating echoed in his eardrums. She was so damned beautiful. Her dark hair was pinned back in a simple chignon and she wore a light green dress that brought out the color of her eyes—made them almost sparkle. Of course that could just be his imagination… "Agatha," he said a little breathlessly. "I was beginning to think I waited in vain."

"Perhaps you have," she said. Her gaze met his and her stubbornness shown through. "I am determined to make this conversation go as quick as possible."

He fought a smile. God he adored this woman. "That's acceptable to me," he said. "We can determine what to do very quickly. Just say yes and then you can go look at your books." He gestured toward the on in her hand. "The duke gave that one back to you."

She glanced down. "I forgot I had it," she answered honestly. "I must have grabbed it off his desk without thinking…" She frowned. "I don't wish to look at it now though." Agatha moved past him and placed the book with the rest of them on the table.

"No?" he said as he studied her. "Why not?"

"Traveling doesn't appeal to me at the moment." Agatha said almost absentmindedly. She didn't turn to meet his gaze as she spoke. "Do you know about everything?"

"That depends," he said carefully. "What is everything? That is a very ambiguous term."

Agatha sighed and walked over toward him and then sat down in the settee. It didn't escape his notice that she hadn't sat directly next to him. She settled in on the far side. "The plot to ruin me," she said and waved her hand dismissively. "You don't have to marry me to save my reputation. I refuse to marry for such a silly reason."

God save him… "And what if I have a better reason than that?"

"There isn't a reason I'll find valid enough to make me agree to tie myself to someone who will have complete control over me for the rest of my life," she said simply. "But please go on. I promised my uncle I'd listen to you."

Her uncle… What had he missed? "Pardon me, can you repeat that last part?"

"About listening to you?" she asked. Agatha tilted her head to the side and studied him. "Would you rather I didn't?"

This was going to be one hell of an uphill battle. He had already fought his own feelings and reasons for staying away from her. Roarke hadn't believed he deserved her, and hell, he didn't. There was a lot of things he wasn't proud of. She was too good for the likes of him. He was fighting for their future though and he wouldn't give in easily. "No, I'm grateful for that. I mean the uncle part. You're speaking of the duke?"

She nodded. "It's a long story, but to make it simple, my mother was his half sister. Now can we move on?"

He would have to ask her more about that later, but it made sense now why she resembled the duke so much. He wouldn't have cared if she was the duke's bastard daughter as many of the ton assumed. Roarke wanted her regardless of her parentage. "Very well," he said. "You wish to discuss the reasons why we should wed."

"Not particularly," she told him. "But I realize you do, so please proceed. Try to convince me." Agatha leaned back against the settee and waited. She didn't look as if anything he said would convince her. Kissing her wouldn't do either, that was what had gotten them in this predicament to begin with.

"Do you know that the baron didn't think anyone, especially me or Riverdale, would marry someone the ton perceived to be a bastard? That's why by some bit of chance you were locked in that room with me." It was perhaps not the best way to begin this argument, but it was where he needed to start. "There was a flaw to that logic of course."

"Oh?" She tilted her head to the side. "And what is that?"

"They didn't take into consideration that I'm obsessed with you," he said.

She jerked back in surprise. "Obsession isn't

healthy."

"I don't always make good decisions," he said. "It's one of my many, many faults. Where you are concerned I've made numerous mistakes over the years."

Agatha lifted a brow. "Should I be aware of all these mistakes?" she asked.

He sighed. She was definitely not making any of this easy. He was fumbling to explain it all to her too. "No," he said softly. "Not all of them. The biggest one though was not courting you properly. You deserved dances, carriage rides, flowers, and all the gifts a proper courtship entails."

"I don't need any of that," she said softly. "Those are just traps I would prefer not to be ensnared with."

His lips twitched. He would not smile and give her another reason to refuse him. "Darling," he began. "Those are not traps. They're meant to honor you."

"I'd rather have something other than flowers," she told him. "Flowers die and then what will I have?"

He laughed then. Roarke couldn't help himself. "So if I showed up at your door with flowers in hand you would refuse them?"

"I would never be so rude." Agatha shook her head. "I do have manners, but that is not what I'm trying to say. It's not your fault," she said. "You just can't be what I need." Agatha closed he eyes and took a deep breath. "I know what you want from me but if we marry you'll wish one day we never met. When that happens a part of me will die. Some things just are not meant to be."

"You're wrong," he said. "I can be everything you need. I want to be and I will." Roarke would not give up. This was far too important. "Together we will be happy. Only apart will we be truly miserable. Don't give up without giving us a chance."

"I don't know…" She glanced away from him.

Roarke took a deep breath. She wasn't openly refusing him now. He might never get her to agree but he had to try. "What can I do or say to make you agree to this."

She shook her head. "Nothing."

He didn't agree. There was something she was waiting for but he hadn't done it or said it. That was why she was still sitting there. She had promised to listen to him and she had. But he hadn't said any of the right things yet. He had to find those words she needed to hear.

She wanted to travel. What if he promised to

take her wherever she wanted to go? Would that garner the yes he coveted so much? No. She would like that but that wasn't what she was waiting for. He knew in that instant what she wanted from him, but his fear of rejection was taking root inside of him. What if she still said no?

He had to try. This was his last chance…

Roarke moved closer. She tried to back up and hit the side of the settee. She had nowhere to go, and she hadn't noticed the mistletoe that had been hung above the settee. This time he'd made sure it had been moved. That temptation would be all he needed to kiss her—but later, not now. He picked up her hand and kissed her palm. "It occurred to me there is one reason I haven't stated. It might just be the one that makes all the difference."

"I'm not sure you've given me any reasons at all. All you have given me is a list of mistakes, but even those aren't that great." Her breathing was a little haggard. His closeness affected her.

"That's true," he said. "So I should give you the only one that will help you decide. It's a big one too."

Roarke rubbed the pad of his thumb over her knuckles. She sucked in a breath. "Then what is it?"

"Look at me," he commanded.

She lifted her gaze and met his. "I'll do anything, fight any battle, or walk any distance for you. I want to spend the rest of my life learning everything there is about you." Her gaze didn't waver once from his. "Once we are married—and we will be married make no mistake about it—we will travel the world. I want you to see everything your heart desires. That curiosity of yours is unquenchable." She licked her lips and he suppressed a groan. Roarke craved her and needed to kiss her again. Soon he promised himself. "And through it all, every hour, every minute, every second of it I promise I'll love you. There won't be one moment of our time together that you will doubt it."

A tear fell down her cheek. "How can you make a promise like that?"

"It's easy," he told her. "Because my heart beats for you. It has since the moment I first met you. I am done fighting what I feel for you." He lifted his hand and wiped the tear from her cheek. "Don't cry angel. It breaks my heart."

"You really love me?" Her voice was hoarse as she spoke.

"I do and I will for the rest of my life. I'll do whatever it takes to make you believe it. If you want to wait and have me court you properly we will. As long as at the end of it you agree to be mine forever. It will be worth it."

"We don't need to do that," she said. Her lips wobbled a little as she attempted to control her tears. "I love you too. I don't want to wait."

Thank heavens… "We belong together," he said. "Always." He gestured for her to look up. "You're under the mistletoe again."

She laughed. "Then you better kiss me before it is moved again."

Roarke chuckled. "I don't need it anymore. You agreed to be mine. I get to kiss you whenever I want now." With that said he leaned down and pressed his lips to hers. He was truly and utterly captivated by this woman. The wedding couldn't happen soon enough for him.

They would have the best life together and he hoped that she would surprise him every day with something new and wonderful. What a blessing this little scheme of the barons had been—Roarke would thank him if not for the evilness behind it.

Agatha had finally agreed to marry him. He'd breathe a sigh of relief if he wasn't too busy kissing her. She was the sweetest, most perfect, woman— and she was all his. He would never let her go…

Thank you so much for taking the time to read my book.

Your opinion matters!

Please take a moment to review this book on your favorite review site and share your opinion with fellow readers.

www.authordawnbrower.com

Excerpt: Disguised as a Wallflower

DAWN BROWER

Lady Seraphina Bell strolled toward a nearby tree on her father, the Duke of Wharton's estate. It was her birthday and she was now three and ten—she been counting down the years until she could be officially launched into society. She craved entertainment and the permission to attend balls, picnics, and soirees. Sera longed to dance… She adored dancing.

She'd been walking and the sun had become unbearable and that tree looked like a wonderful spot to take a respite. So she'd decided to rest under the shade for a little while. If she were brave enough she would consider walking a little farther to the little pond and swim. She would have to undress though and that would be most improper.

Should she dare to anyway? Her father wouldn't approve at all.

She nibbled on her bottom lip. There was no one around and Sebastian wasn't supposed to return for a few days. Her father had informed her of that earlier that day. He was also bringing friends with him. Two of his closest school chums. Sera was glad that her cousin was making friends. He had a difficult time at school and some of the meaner boys had picked on him.

After careful consideration she decided to go to the pond. It was unusually hot and she wanted to take a swim. Her father would forgive her the impropriety. He might not like it, but he was never horrid to her. All she would get was a long stern lecture from her. If she had been born a boy this wouldn't even be a concern. But no, she'd been born female, and that made the rules far more strict for her. She wrinkled her nose. Sometimes it truly was abysmal to be a girl, but she did so love dresses. That made up for some of the worst aspects of being female.

She rushed toward the pond. Once she reached the water she slipped offer shoes. She sat down and removed her stockings and struggled to undo her ties in the back of her dress. "Drat," she said in a soft tone.

"What are you doing?"

She froze. That was a decidedly male tone, and not one she was familiar with. Sera turned to glance at toward the sound and sucked in a breath. He was…beautiful. His hair was a rich golden blond kissed by the sun. The locks were thick and she wanted to run her fingers through them to see if they were as soft as they appeared to be. As gorgeous as his hair was—that said nothing about his eyes. They were an ice blue. So cold they made her shiver instinctively.

"Who are you?" she said in her most prim tone.

He lifted a brow. "I'm the Duke of Riverdale. You should address me as Your Grace."

"Should I?" she lifted a brow. "And why would I do that?" Her father was a duke and she knew the proper etiquette, but something screamed at her not to give in to this beautiful boy. He was perhaps a few years older than her—maybe seven and ten. She could be wrong though. Was this one of Bas's friends?

"Because I'm a duke," he sputtered.

"And?" she smirked at him. "I'm a duke's daughter. You are not that special."

He furrowed his eyebrows together. "You're quite rude."

"Thank you," she said in a smug tone. "Then I do believe I'm done here." Sera stood and bent over to collect her shoes, but slipped and went tumbling into the water.

She sputtered and flailed in the pond. It was much deeper than she remembered and her dress was making it difficult for her to swim. She struggled but still began to sink despite her efforts.

"I suppose you think I should save you now," the duke said in a aggravated tone.

She couldn't very well answer the aggravating duke to do that when she was fighting for her life. If she made it out of the water she was going to smack him hard. How dare he mock her when she might die. She popped to the surface again and noticed him pulling off his boots. He tossed them to the side and dived in. He swam over to her with ease, but she had somehow managed to remain afloat.

"I don't need you," she spat at him.

He sighed heavily. "You're the most contrary female…"

"Go away," she said and tried to move past him. He didn't allow her to though.

"Don't be difficult. You're not going to be able

to swim in that gown." He wrapped an arm around her waist and dragged her to shore, then picked her up and tossed her onto the muddy bank. Her hip hit hard and she moaned as the pain shot through her. He was so bloody awful.

"And you called me rude," she said as she spit pond water out of her mouth. Why had she thought swimming would be a grand idea. "Why are you here anyway."

The Duke of Riverdale pulled himself out of the pond and slid down next to her. "I didn't plan on this impromptu swim that's for certain." He wiped a hand over his wet blond locks. It didn't look as silky as before but that didn't make him less appealing. If anything those wet clothes made him…far more attractive. She could see, well, everything. That led to some very unladylike thoughts. If her father could see inside her head he'd send her someplace to make here rethink everything.

Why him? He was horrid. She'd never laid eyes upon anyone and instantly been attracted to them. "That doesn't tell me anything." She glared at him. "Are you going to answer me?"

"No," he said. "I don't think I will." He stood then picked up his boots. "I trust you can find your own way back or is that too much for you too."

Oh… She wanted to throw something at him, but there was nothing easily on hand. She'd give anything for a stone, hell a pebble. Something. "I hate you."

"Back at you sweetheart," he said in a droll tone. The duke saluted her and then left her alone at the pond. He had to be Bas's friend. She would have a long talk with her cousin when she saw him. He had terrible taste in friends… Sera hoped she never saw the rude duke again.

Order here: www.books2read.com/
Disguisedasawallflower

Acknowledgments

Special thanks to Elizabeth Evans. Your encouragement and assistance with this book helped me immensely. I am grateful for all you do for me.

About Dawn Brower

USA TODAY Bestselling author, DAWN BROWER writes both historical and contemporary romance. There are always stories inside her head; she just never thought she could make them come to life. That creativity has finally found an outlet.

Growing up, she was the only girl out of six children. She raised two boys as a single mother; there is never a dull moment in her life. Reading books is her favorite hobby, and she loves all genres.

www.authordawnbrower.com
TikTok: @1DawnBrower

BB bookbub.com/authors/dawn-brower
f facebook.com/1DawnBrower
🐦 twitter.com/1DawnBrower
O instagram.com/1DawnBrower
g goodreads.com/dawnbrower

Also by Dawn Brower

HISTORICAL

Stand alone:

Broken Pearl

A Wallflower's Christmas Kiss

A Gypsy's Christmas Kiss

Marsden Romances

A Flawed Jewel

A Crystal Angel

A Treasured Lily

A Sanguine Gem

A Hidden Ruby

A Discarded Pearl

Marsden Descendants

Rebellious Angel

Tempting An American Princess

How to Kiss a Debutante

Loving an America Spy

Linked Across Time

Saved by My Blackguard

Searching for My Rogue

Seduction of My Rake

Surrendering to My Spy

Spellbound by My Charmer

Stolen by My Knave

Separated from My Love

Scheming with My Duke

Secluded with My Hellion

Secrets of My Beloved

Spying on My Scoundrel

Shocked by My Vixen

Smitten with My Christmas Minx

Vision of Love

Enduring Legacy

The Legacy's Origin

Charming Her Rogue

Ever Beloved

Forever My Earl

Always My Viscount

Infinitely My Marquess

Eternally My Duke

Bluestockings Defying Rogues

When An Earl Turns Wicked

A Lady Hoyden's Secret

One Wicked Kiss

Earl In Trouble

All the Ladies Love Coventry

One Less Scandalous Earl

Confessions of a Hellion

The Vixen in Red

Lady Pear's Duke

Scandal Meets Love

Love Only Me (Amanda Mariel)

Find Me Love (Dawn Brower)

If It's Love (Amanda Mariel)

Odds of Love (Dawn Brower)

Believe In Love (Amanda Mariel)

Chance of Love (Dawn Brower)

Love and Holly (Amanda Mariel)

Love and Mistletoe (Dawn Brower

The Neverhartts

Never Defy a Vixen

Never Disregard a Wallflower

Never Dare a Hellion

Never Deceive a Bluestocking

Never Disrespect a Governess

Never Desire a Duke

CONTEMPORARY

Stand alone:

Deadly Benevolence

Snowflake Kisses

Kindred Lies

Sparkle City

Diamonds Don't Cry

Hooking a Firefly

Novak Springs

Cowgirl Fever

Dirty Proof

Unbridled Pursuit

Sensual Games

Christmas Temptation

Daring Love

Passion and Lies

Desire and Jealousy

Seduction and Betrayal

Begin Again

There You'll Be

Better as a Memory

Won't Let Go

Heart's Intent

One Heart to Give

Unveiled Hearts

Heart of the Moment

Kiss My Heart Goodbye

Heart in Waiting

Heart Lessons

A Heart Redeemed

Kismet Bay

Once Upon a Christmas

New Year Revelation

All Things Valentine

Luck At First Sight

Endless Summer Days

A Witch's Charm

All Out of Gratitude

Christmas Ever After

YOUNG ADULT FANTASY

Broken Curses

The Enchanted Princess

The Bespelled Knight

The Magical Hunt

www.ingramcontent.com/pod-product-compliance
Lightning Source LLC
Chambersburg PA
CBHW051832130726
47987CB00002B/506